AF594807

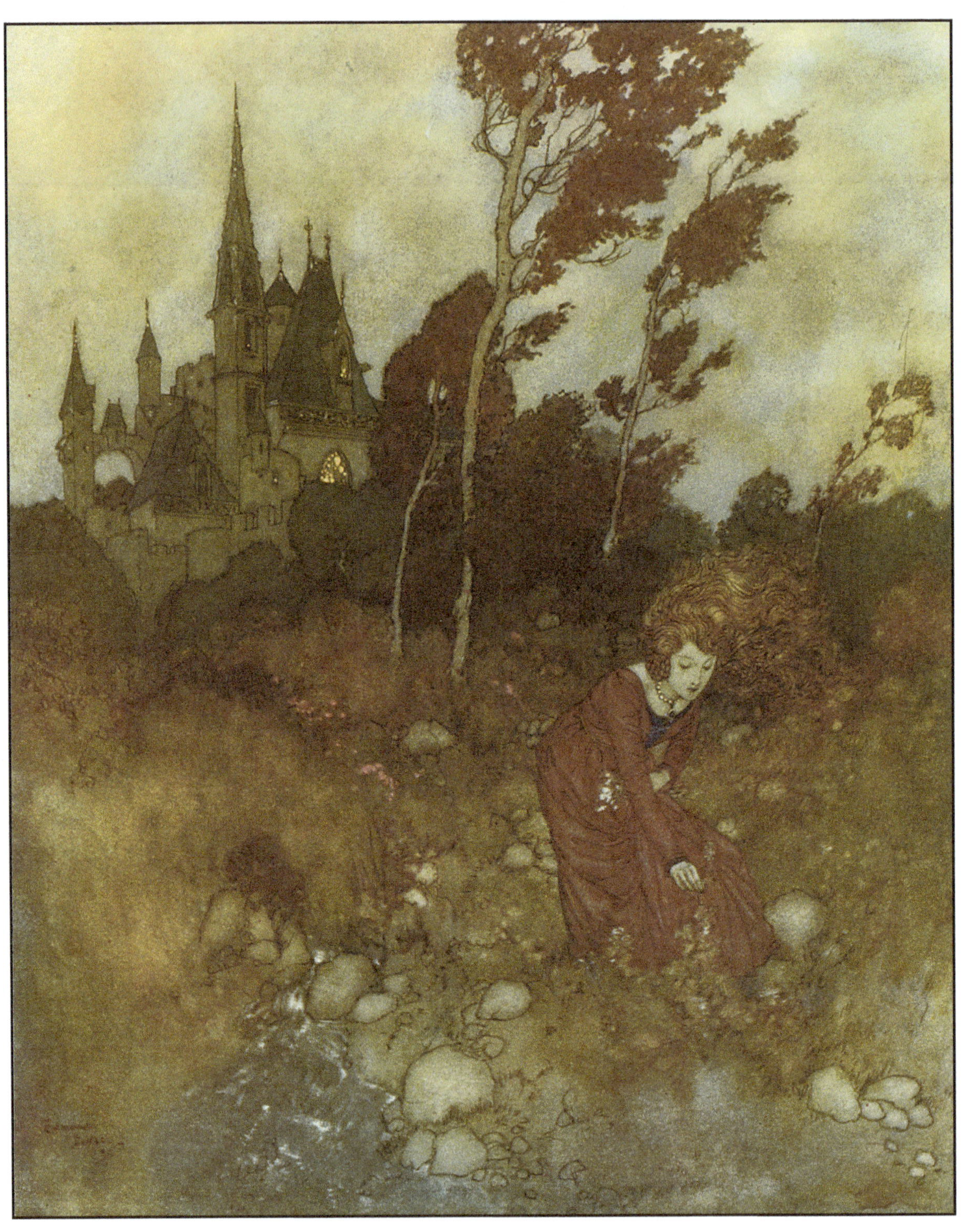

I used to meet her in the garden, the ravine, and in the manor fields. She was always picking flowers and herbs, those she knew her father could use for healing drinks and potions.
From "The Wind's Tale"

Dulac's Fairy Tale Illustrations
IN FULL COLOR

Selected and Edited by Jeff A. Menges

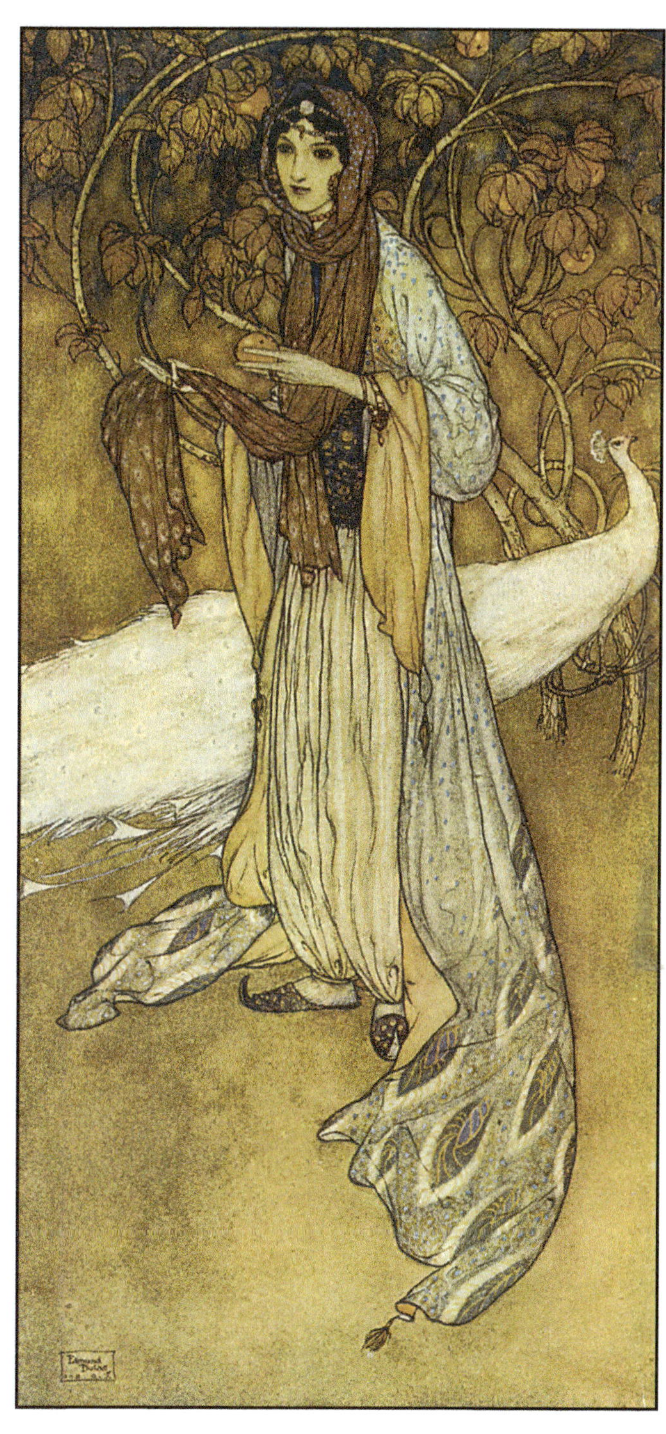

Princess Scheherazade, The Heroine of the Thousand-and-one nights, ranks among the greatest storytellers of the world
From "Tales of the Arabian Nights"

Dover Publications, Garden City, New York

This Dover edition, first published in 2004, is an original compilation of illustrations from the following works: *The Sleeping Beauty and Other Fairy Tales* (published by Hodder & Stoughton, Ltd., London, 1910); *Stories from Hans Andersen* (published by Hodder & Stoughton, Ltd., London, 1911); *Princess Badoura* (published by Hodder & Stoughton, Ltd., London, 1913); *Sindbad the Sailor and Other Stories from the Arabian Nights* (published by Hodder & Stoughton, Ltd., London, 1914); *Edmund Dulac's Fairy Book* (published by Hodder & Stoughton, Ltd., London, 1916); *Stories from the Arabian Nights* (published by Hodder & Stoughton, Ltd., London, 1916); and *Edmund Dulac's Picture Book* (Hodder & Stoughton, Ltd., London, 1916).

Library of Congress Cataloging-in-Publication Data

Dulac, Edmund, 1882–1953.
Dulac's fairy tale illustrations in full color / selected and edited by Jeff A. Menges.
p. cm.
ISBN-13: 978-0-486-43669-2 (pbk.)
ISBN-10: 0-486-43669-1 (pbk.)
1. Dulac, Edmund, 1882–1953. 2. Fairy tales—Illustrations. I. Title: Fairy tale illustrations in full color. II. Menges, Jeff A. III. Title.

NC978.5.D84A4 2004
741.6'4'092—dc22

2004052694

Printed in Canada
43669115 2026
www.doverpublications.com

Introduction

Edmund Dulac is remembered most for the body of work he produced during a single decade of his life at the start of his artistic career. Born in Toulouse, France, in 1882, Dulac displayed an interest in art at an early age. He had a passion for the exotic, notably the artistic styles and stories of distant lands. This appetite was nurtured by the artwork and prints that his father brought home from his travels for young Edmund to study. He also loved the works of English artist–illustrators, such as Walter Crane, William Morris, and Aubrey Beardsley. To see the dazzlingly detailed characters and settings in the visionary art of Edmund Dulac, it is hard to fathom that he had finished his second year of law school before committing himself to becoming an illustrator.

At the start of the twentieth century, new developments in printing technology made color reproductions available at a reasonable cost for the first time. Thus was born a demand for color illustrators, and the new industry flourished. In the autumn of 1904, newly settled into London from France, the 22-year-old French illustrator launched his search for magazine work. After only a few weeks in London, displaying an incredible eagerness and an armful of drawings, Dulac was hired by publisher J. M. Dent to provide sixty color pieces to illustrate the complete works of the Brontë sisters. *Jane Eyre* was his first volume, and the twelve pieces in this group were well received, sending Dulac on his way to becoming one of the premier artists of the Golden Age of book illustration.

During the Christmas season of 1905, William Heinemann, a prominent London publishing house, signed Arthur Rackham to illustrate a gift-book edition of Washington Irving's *Rip Van Winkle.* The book had fifty-five color plates, and was a tremendous success for both artist and publisher. Hodder and Stoughton, Heinemann's biggest competitor, decided to compete on this new level, and Dulac was the right person for the job. In an unusual arrangement with Liecester Galleries, Hodder and Stoughton signed Dulac, who went on to produce gift books for them annually for the next ten years. It is this body of work that the present volume examines—specifically, the variety of fairy tale illustrations done by Dulac during the Hodder and Stoughton years. Edmund Dulac was the perfect artist to explore the mysterious, romantic tales of the *Arabian Nights* and *Sindbad;* his delicate line work and jewel-toned palette bring to life Hans Christian Andersen's tales.

As a result of the publication of these books, Dulac's artistic growth and reputation both flourished. It seemed as if his future was set, but World War I put an end to this annual routine. Paper had become a premium during the war, and publishing outside of the war effort was significantly curtailed. In the years during the war, Dulac's work appeared in a number of books sponsored to raise money for the war effort. These years were a great strain on both Dulac and his wife, both mentally and financially.

Toward the war's end, as well as afterward, Dulac became involved with a number of theatrical productions, doing scenery and costume designs. In 1918 he produced what would be his last book for Hodder and Stoughton, Nathaniel Hawthorne's *Tanglewood Tales.* Book illustration in the style for which Dulac was known was much less in demand, forcing him to find work in other areas of the graphic arts. His later endeavors included caricature, portraiture, package design, and a good deal of work in stamp and bank note design. From 1924 until 1949, he had an association with Hearst Newspapers' *The American Weekly,* from which he earned the majority of his income at that time. Dulac was actively working up until his death in 1953.

Jeff A. Menges
May 2004

For Jenny

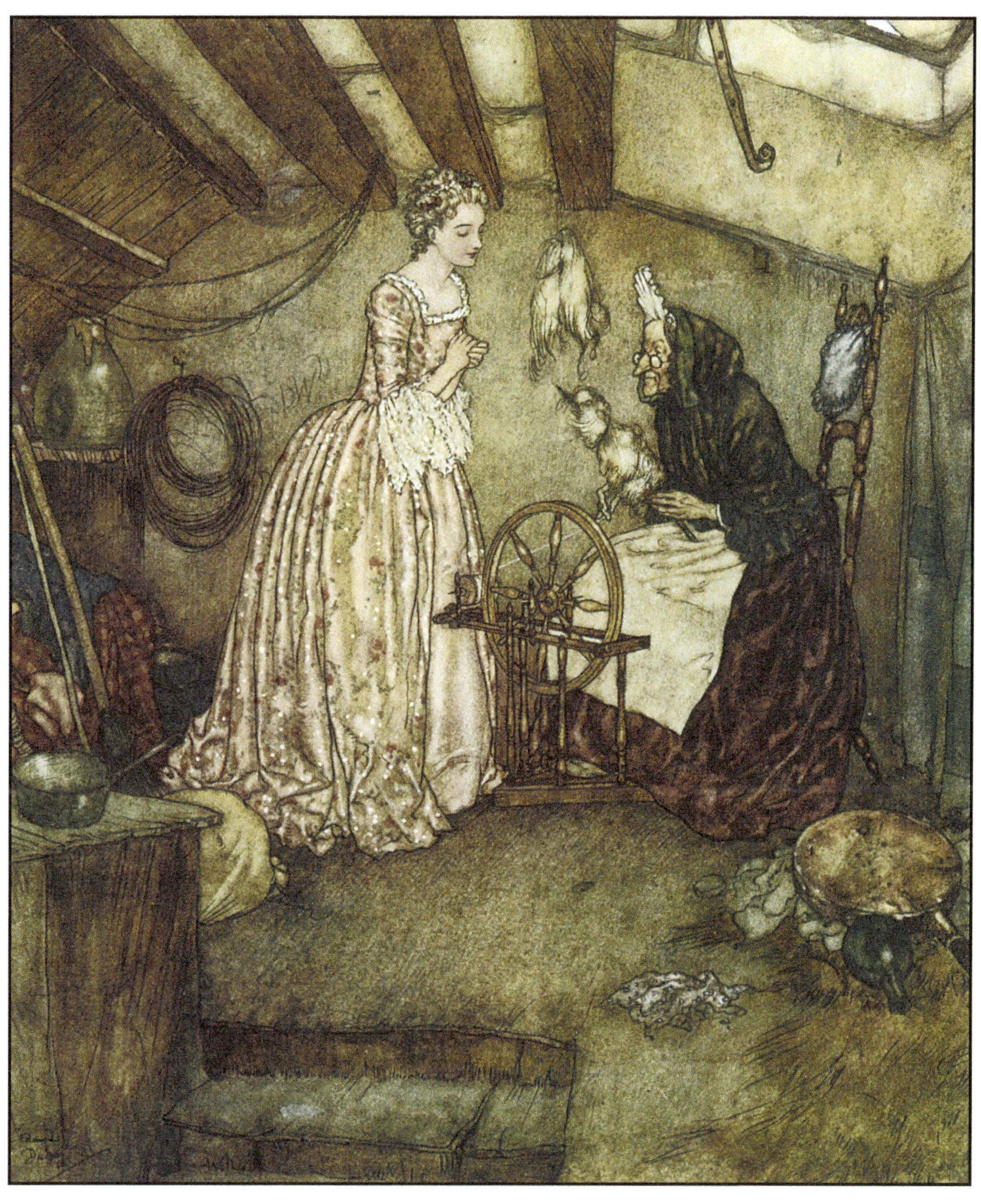

"I am spinning, the pretty one," answered the old woman,
who did not know who she was.
From "The Sleeping Beauty"

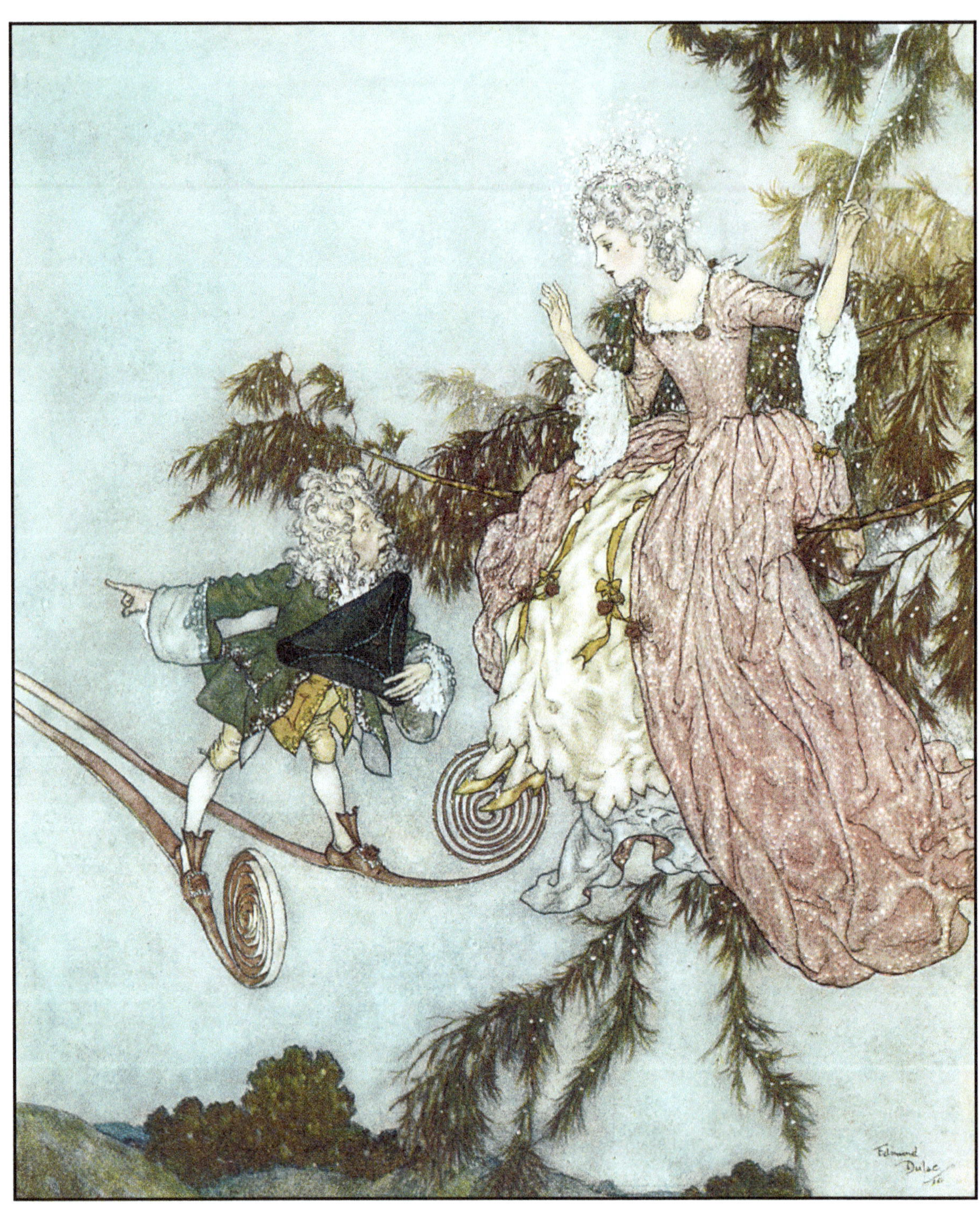

But news of it was brought to her by a little dwarf,
who owned a pair of seven-league boots.
From "The Sleeping Beauty"

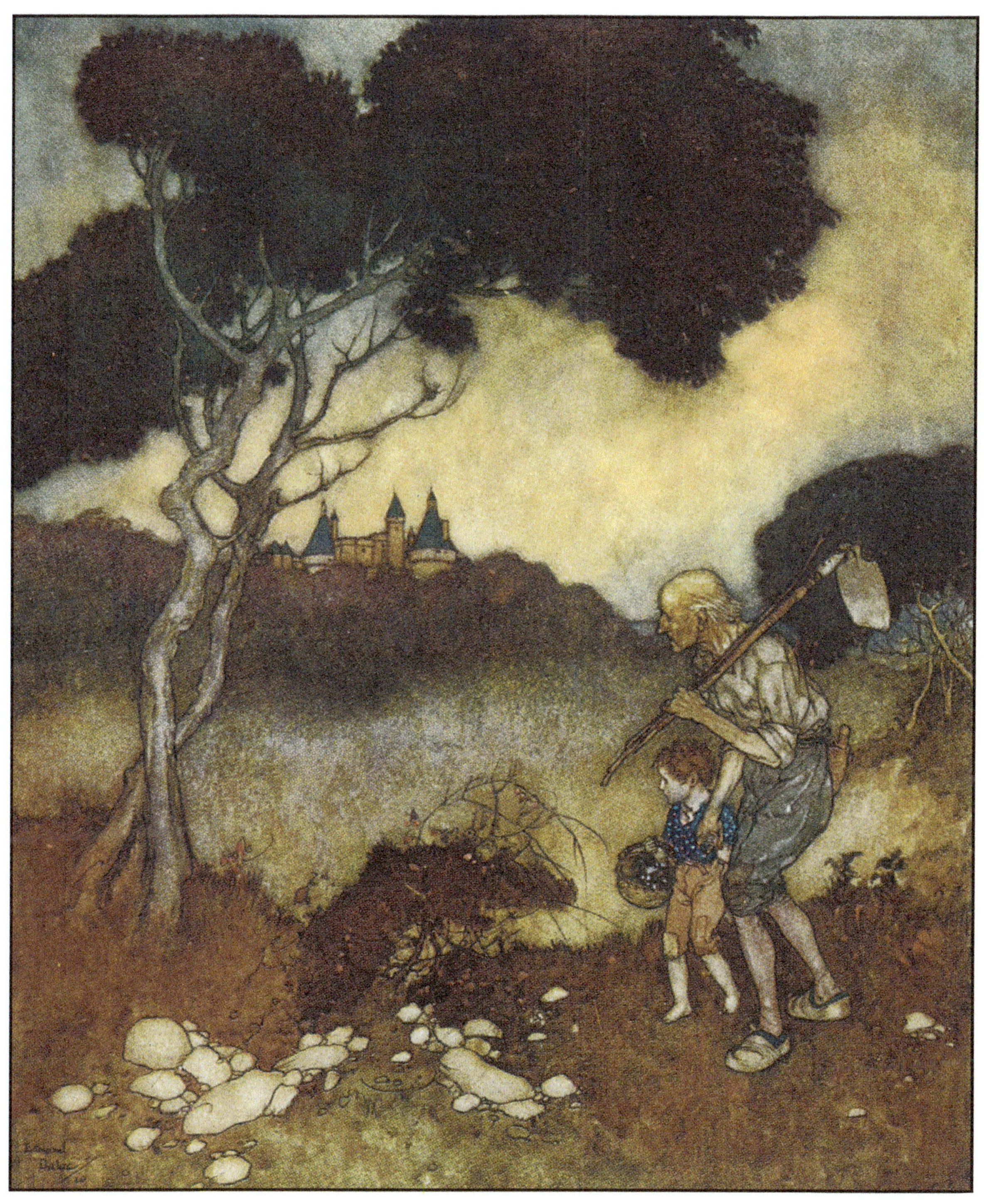

They grew until nothing but the tops of the castle towers could be seen.
From "The Sleeping Beauty"

Plate 3

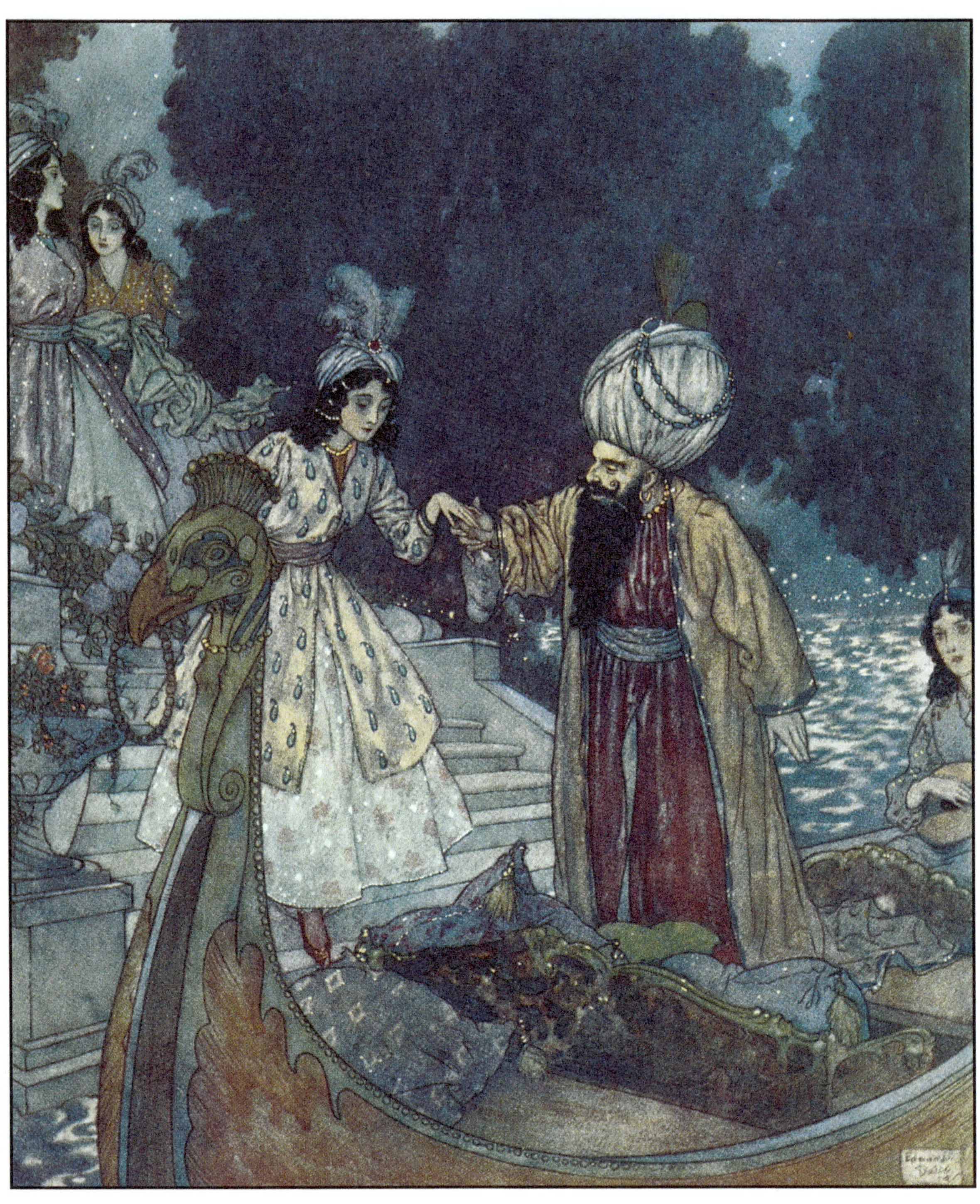

They were rowed to the sound of music on the waters
of their host's private canal.
From "Blue Beard"

Plate 4

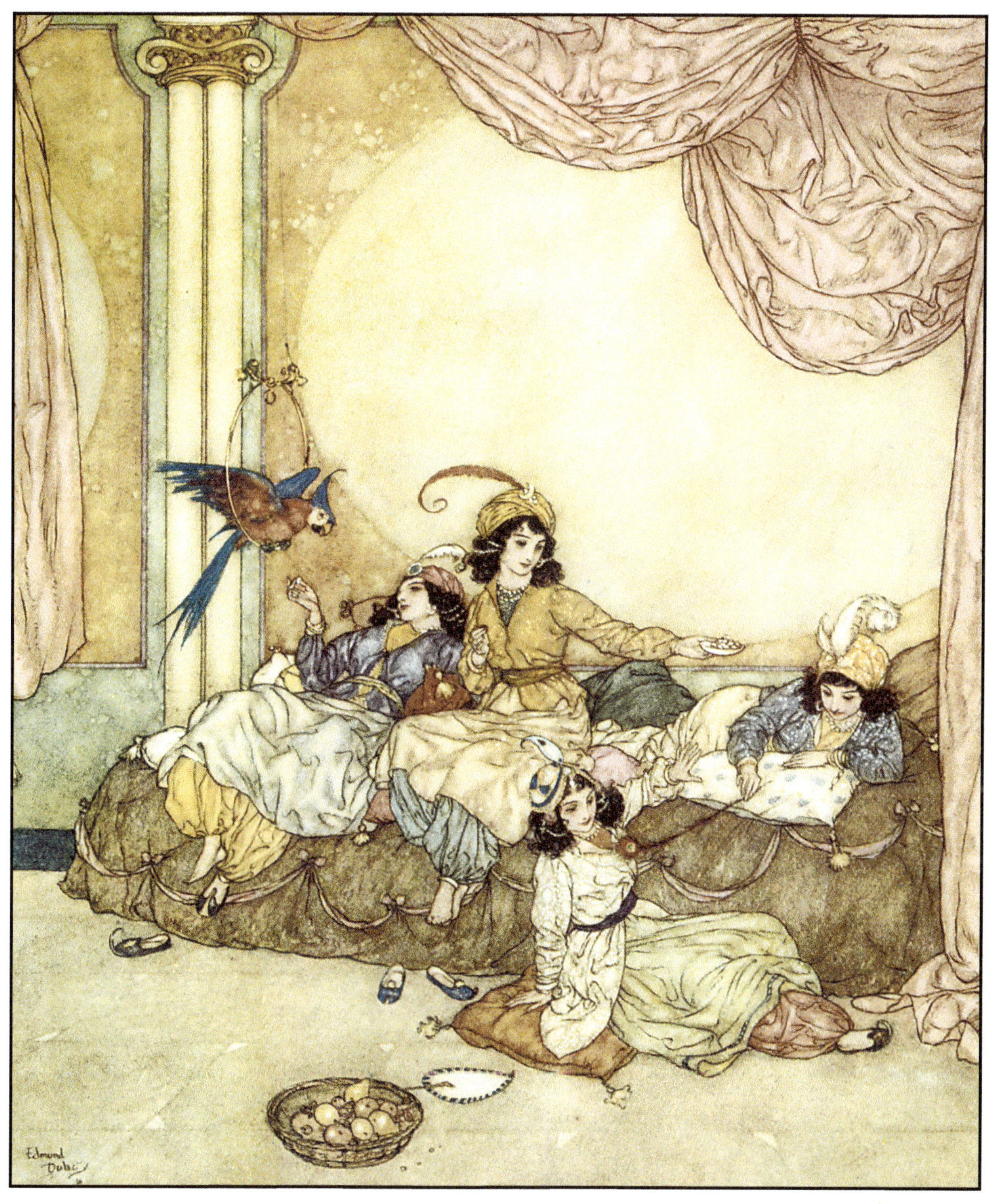

They overran the house with loss of time.
From "Blue Beard"

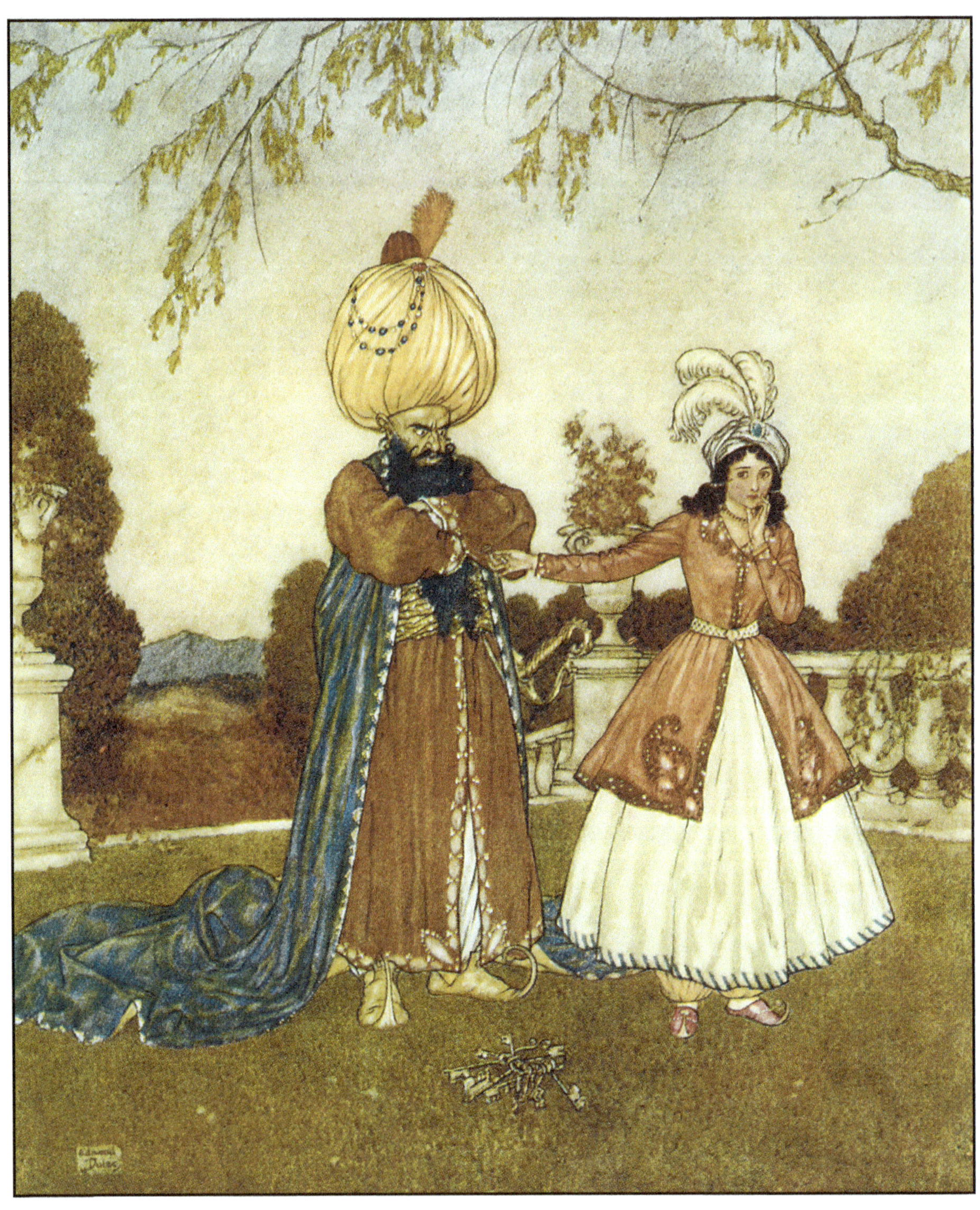

"You SHALL go in, and take your place among the ladies
you saw there!"
From "Blue Beard"

Plate 6

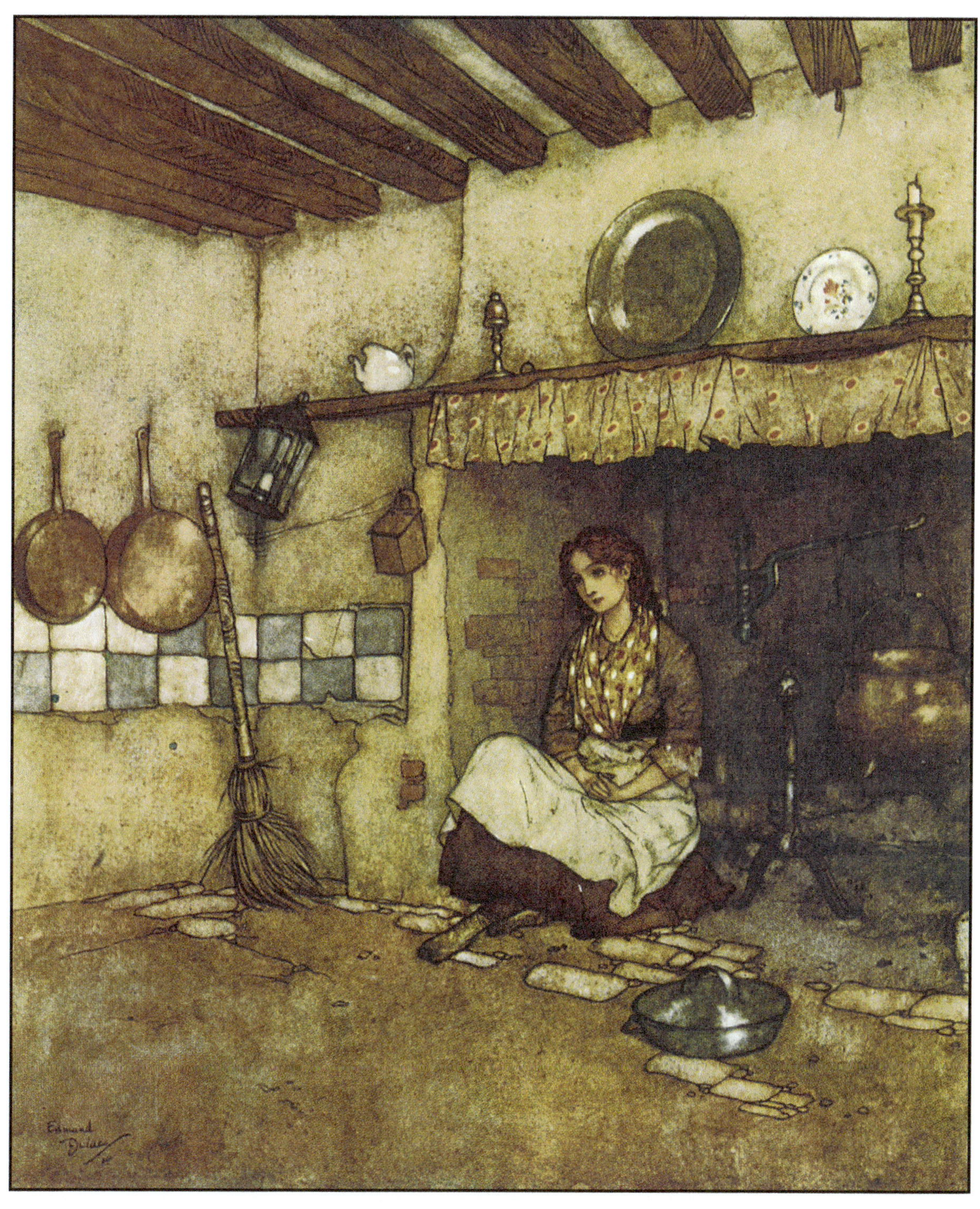

She used to creep away to the chimney-corner
and seat herself among the cinders.
From "Cinderella"

Plate 7

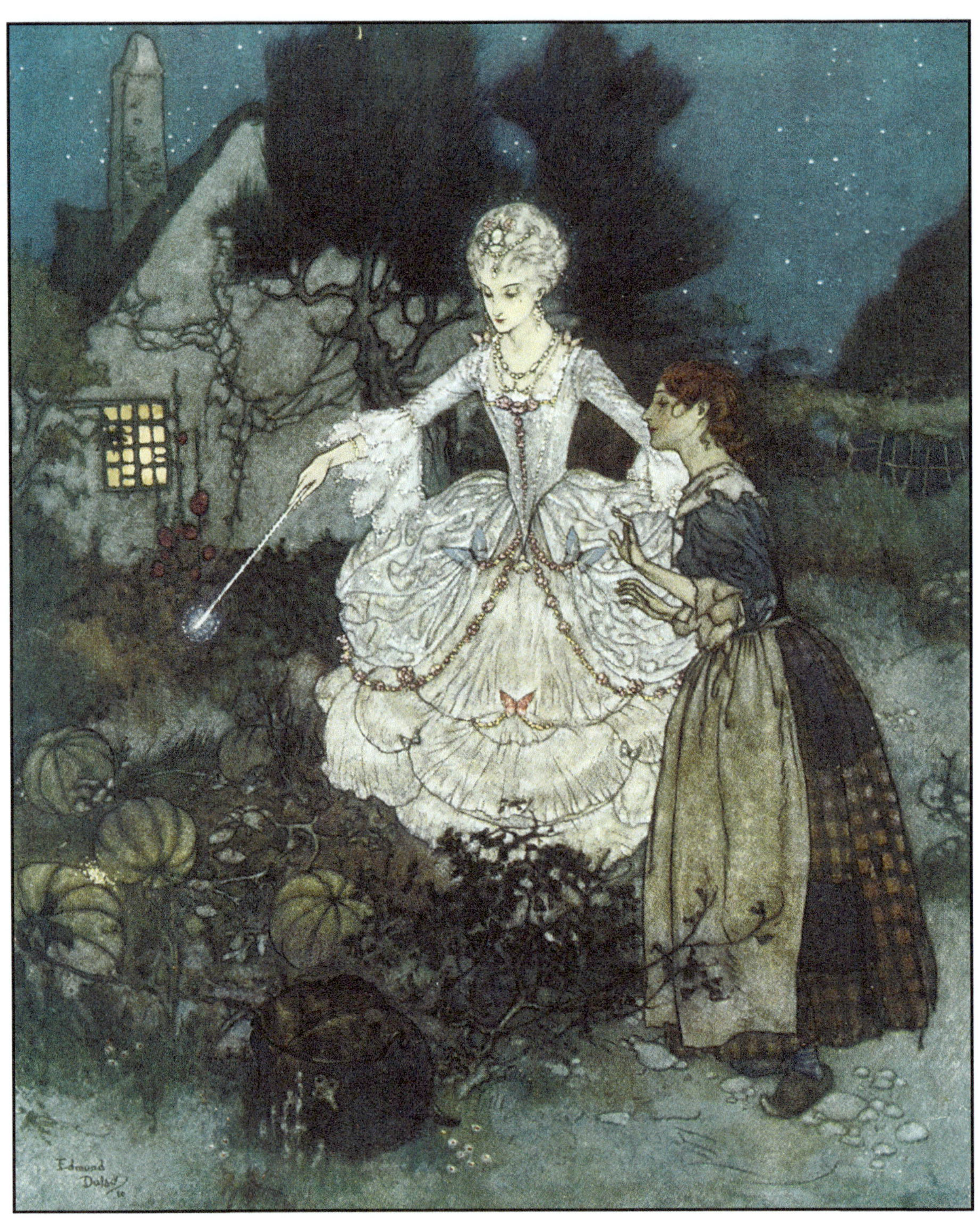

And her Godmother pointed to the finest of all
with her wand.
From "Cinderella"

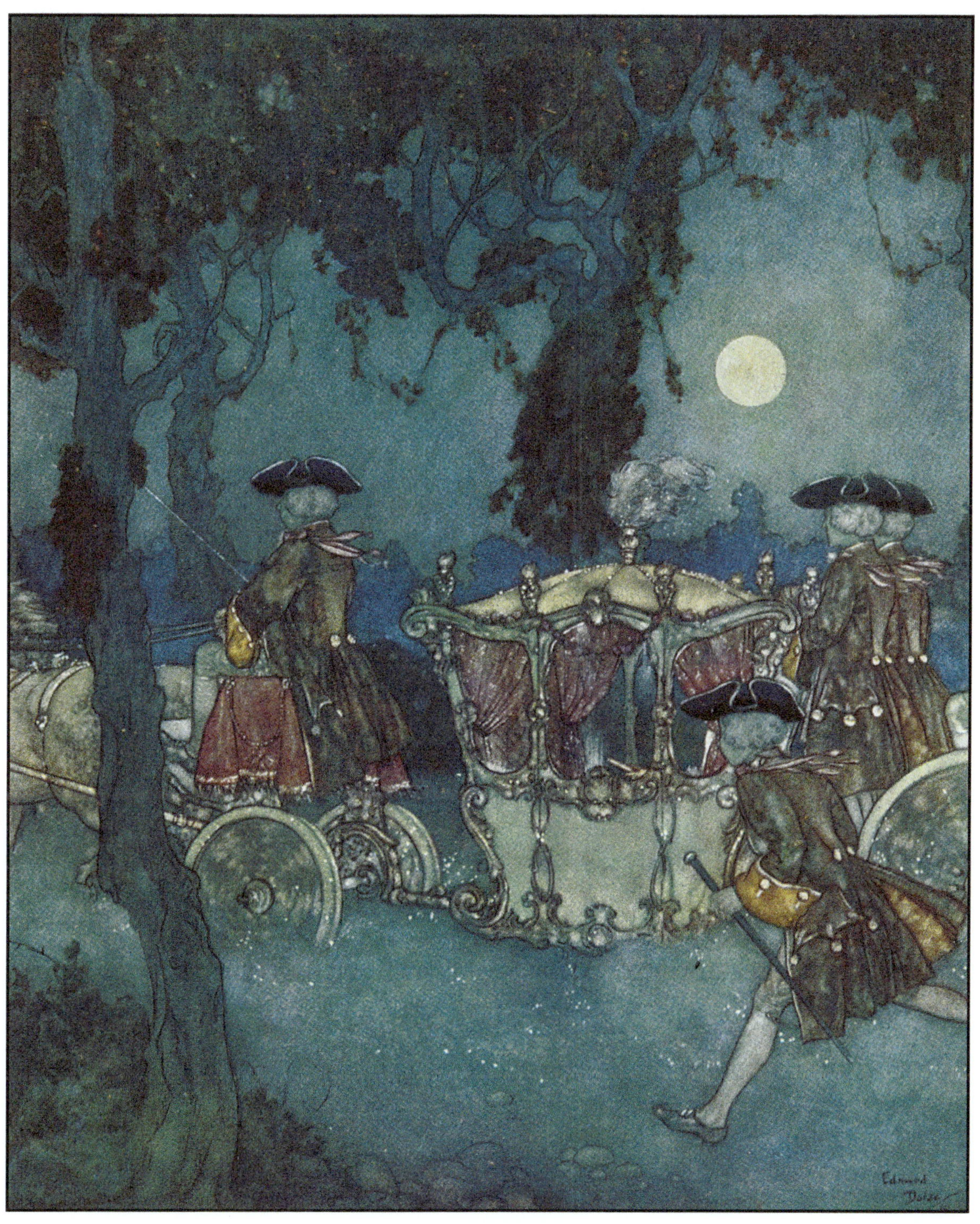

She was driven away, beside herself with Joy.
From "Cinderella"

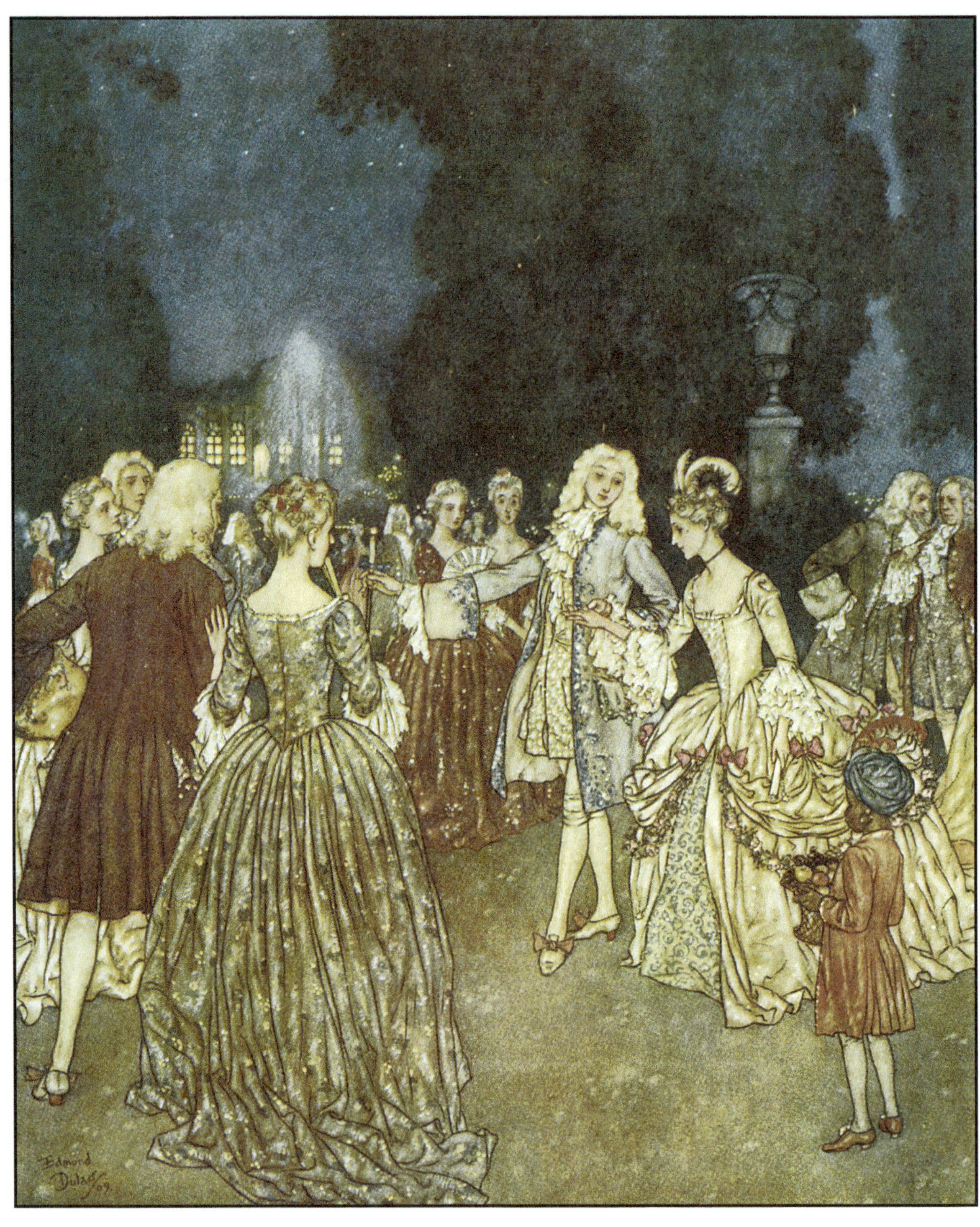

The King's son led her through the gardens, where the guests drew apart and gazed in wonder at her loveliness.
From "Cinderella"

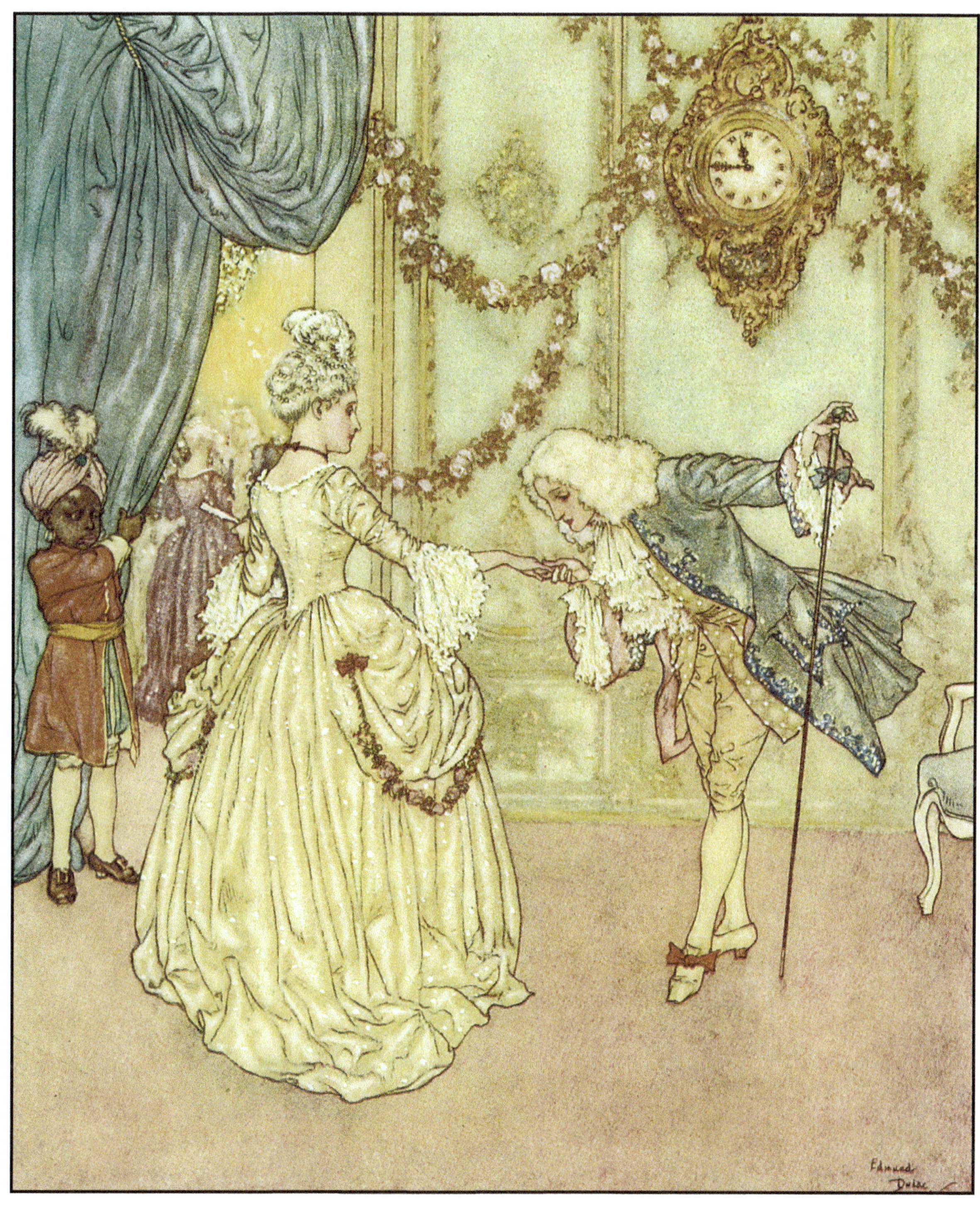

Whereupon she instantly desired her partner to lead her to the King and Queen.
From "Cinderella"

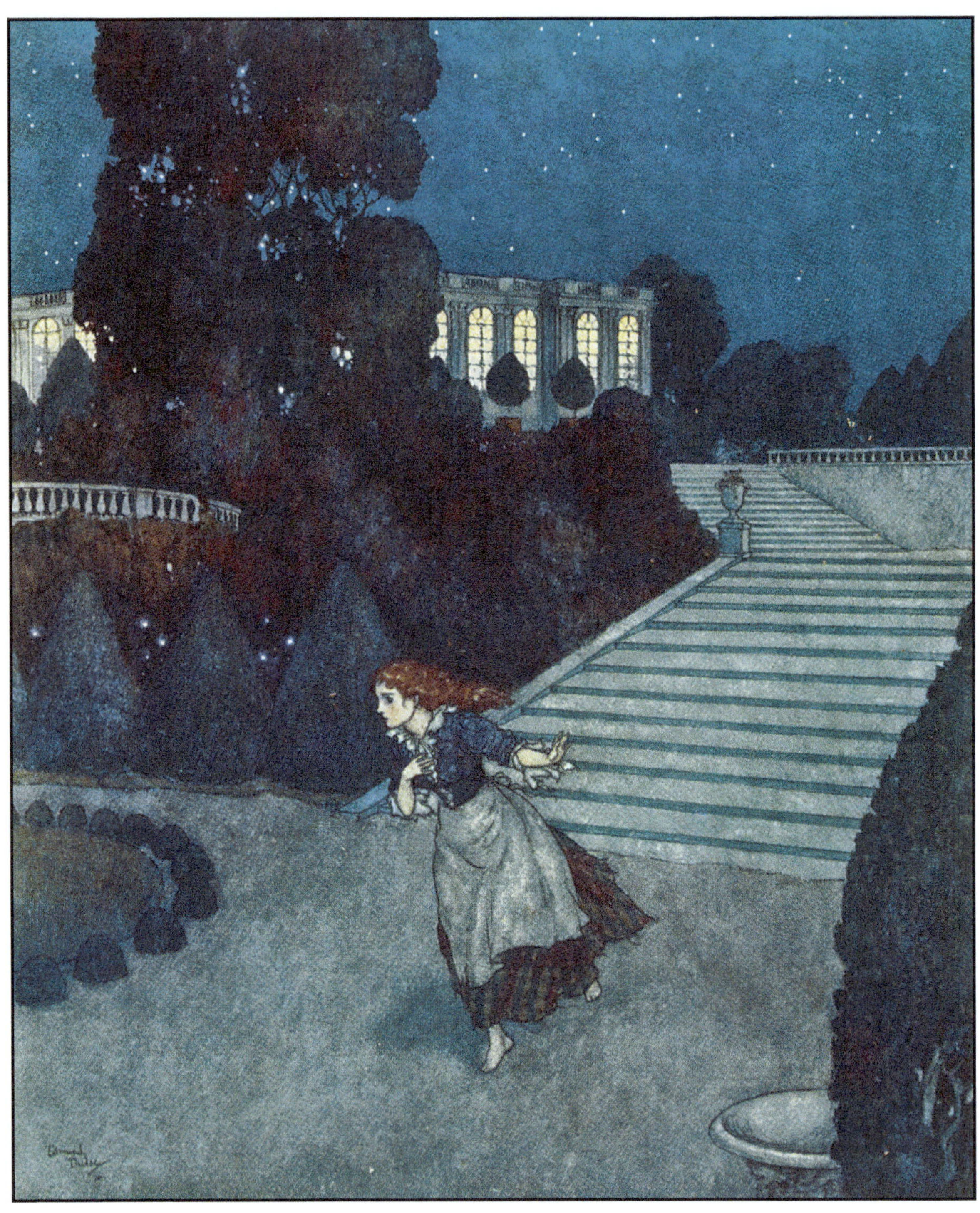

She made her escape as lightly as a deer.
From "Cinderella"

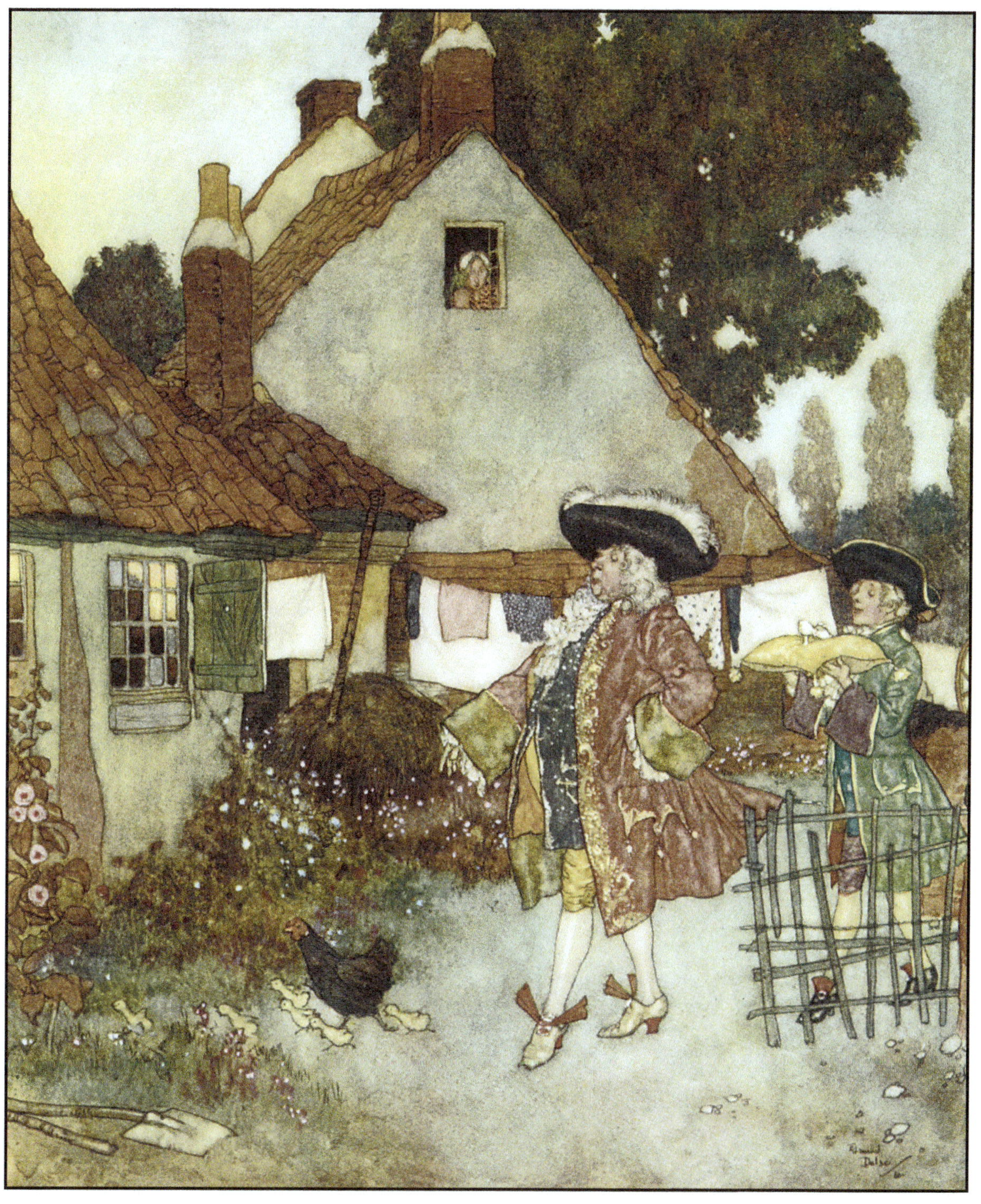

The Prime Minister was kept very busy for the next few weeks.
From "Cinderella"

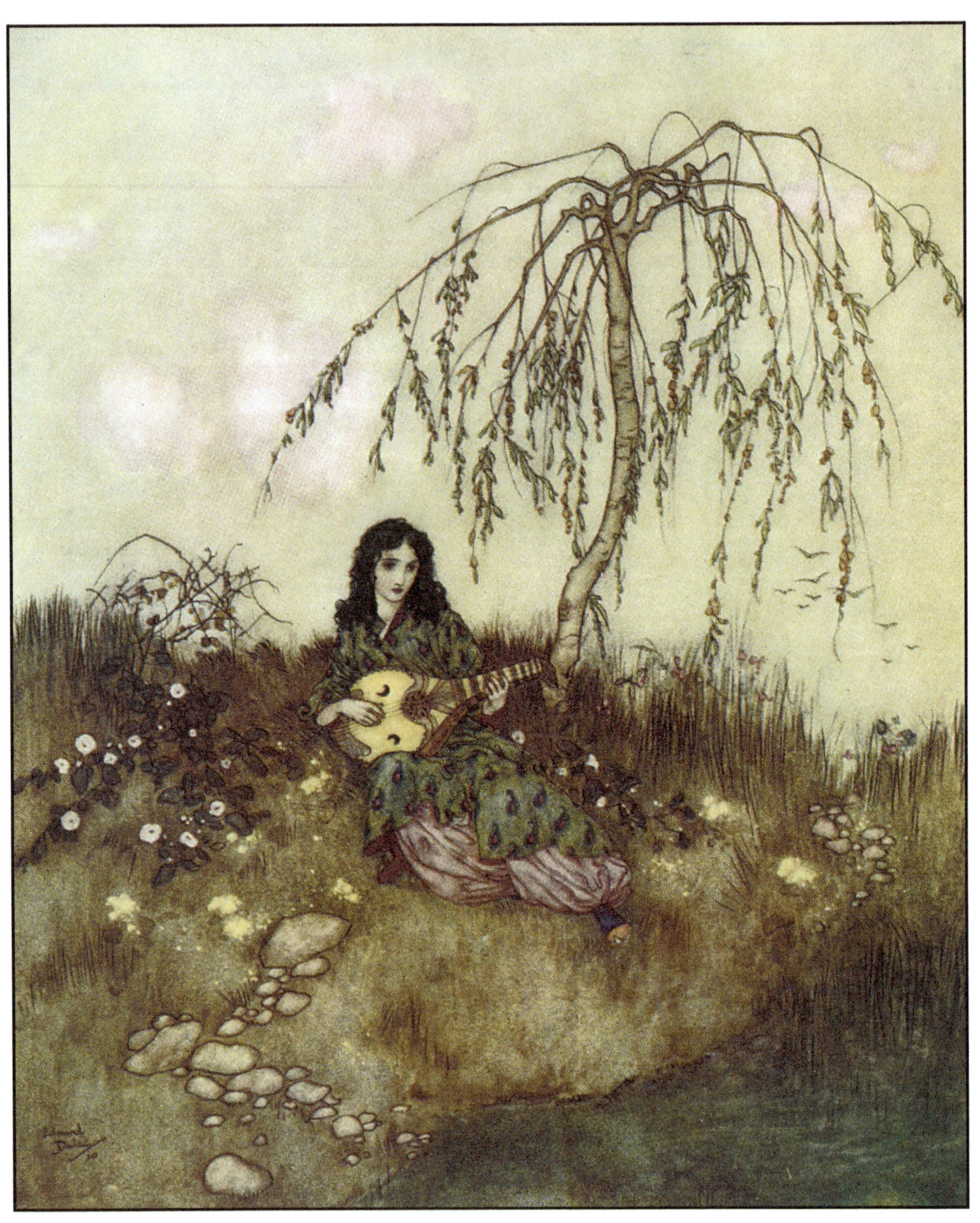

After she had done her work, [she] would sing and play.
From "Beauty and the Beast"

Plate 14

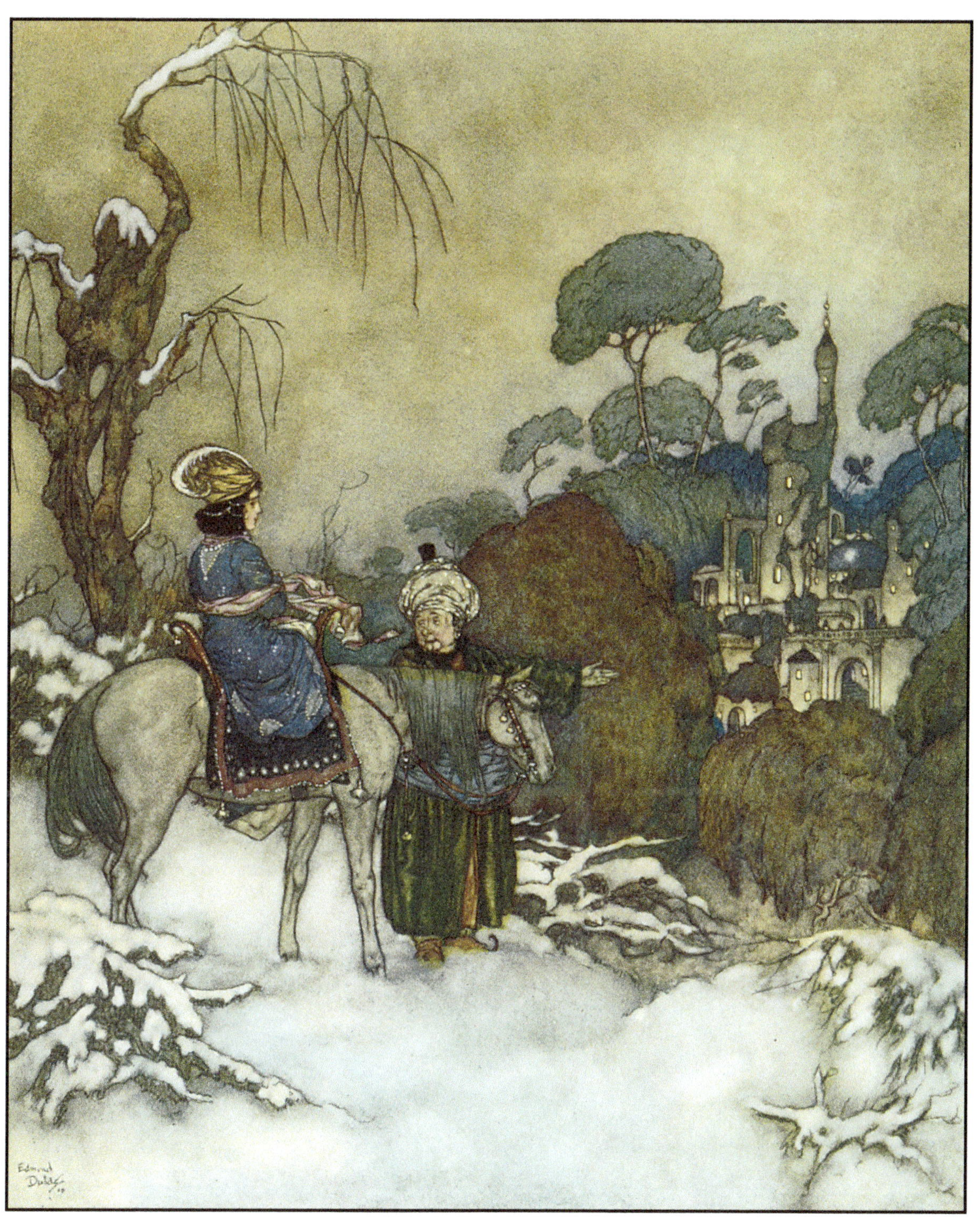

Soon they caught sight of the castle in the distance.
From "Beauty and the Beast"

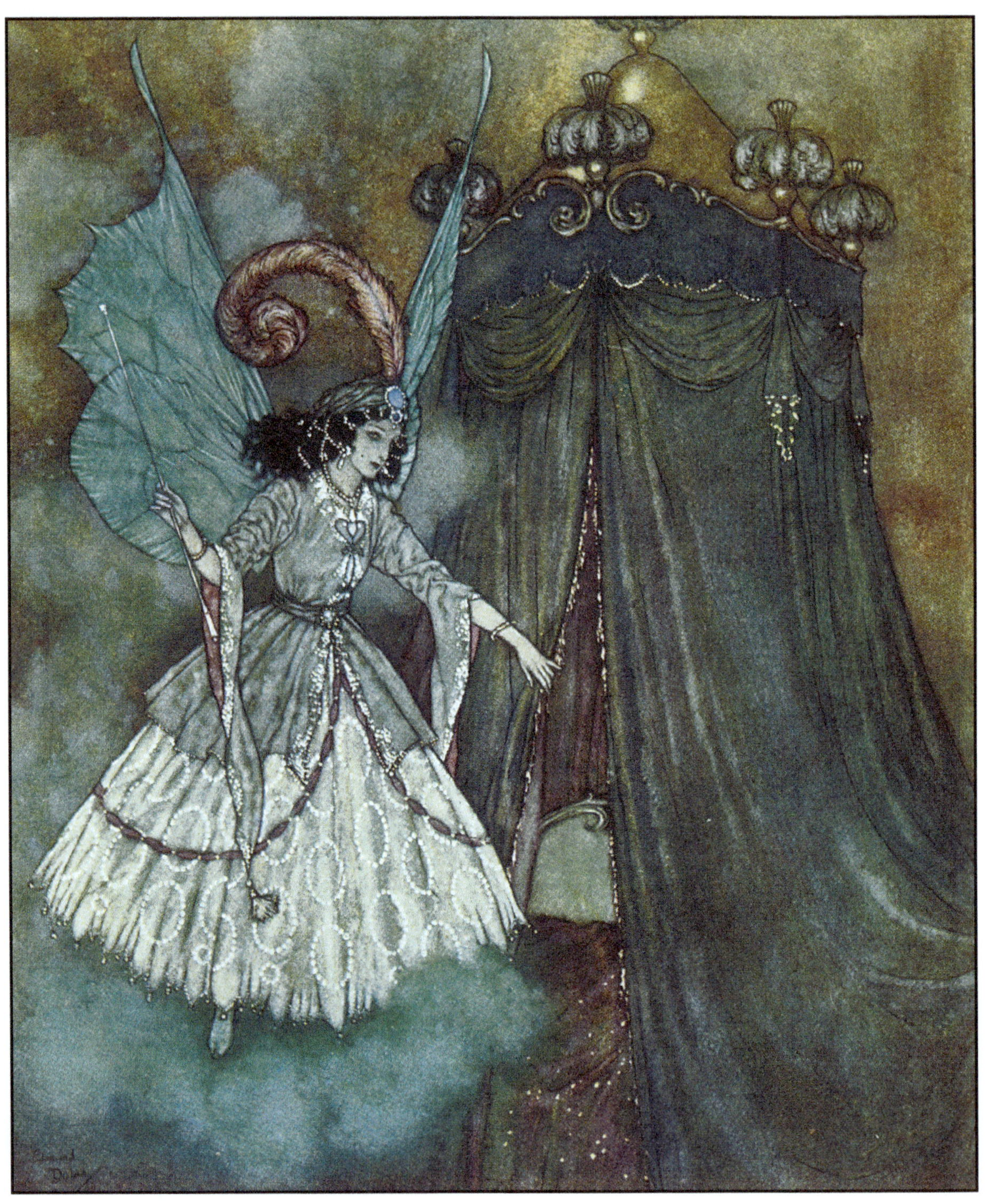

She found herself face to face with a stately and beautiful lady.
From "Beauty and the Beast"

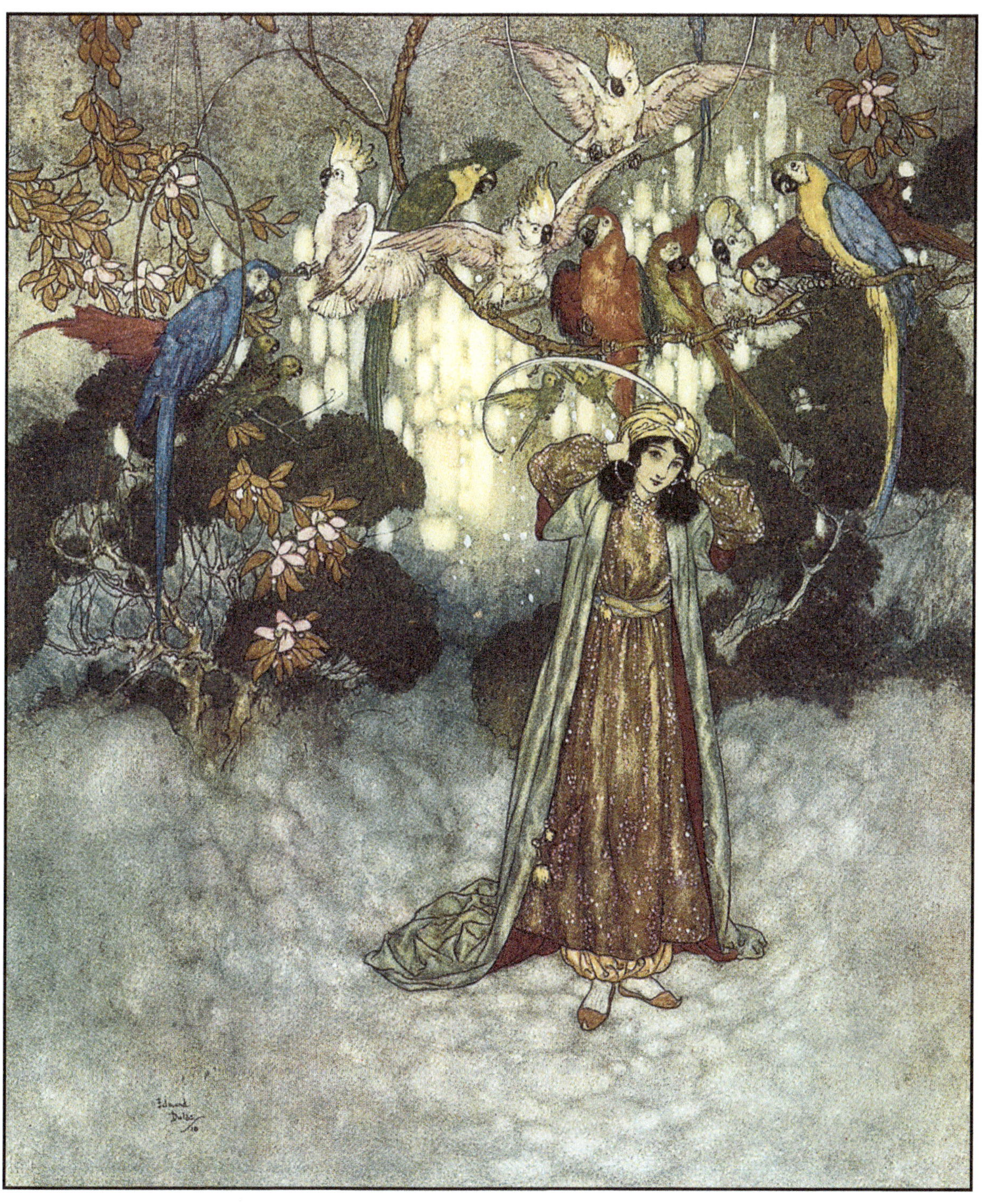

These no sooner saw Beauty than they began to scream and chatter.
From "Beauty and the Beast"

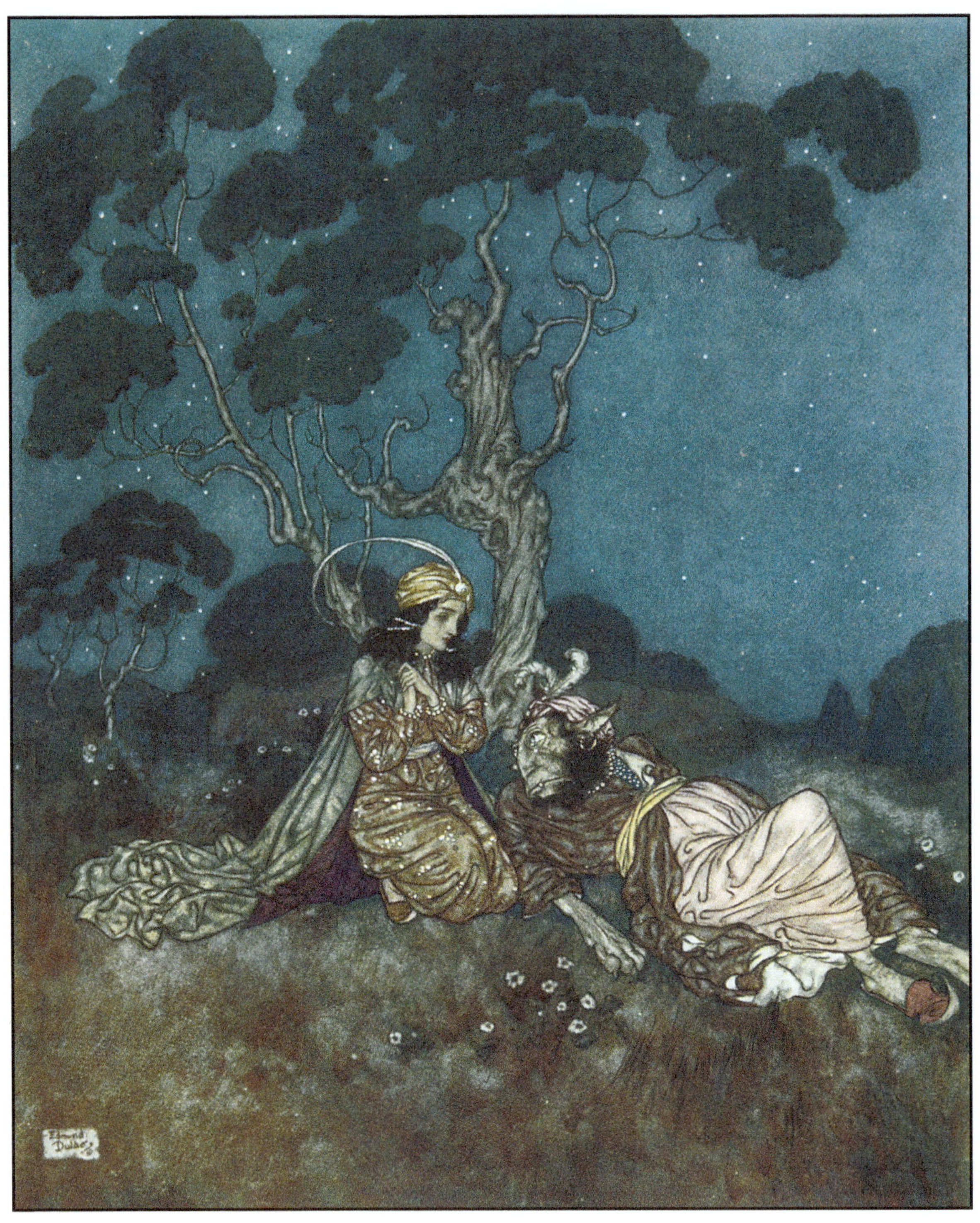

"Ah! what a fright you have given me!" she murmured.
From "Beauty and the Beast"

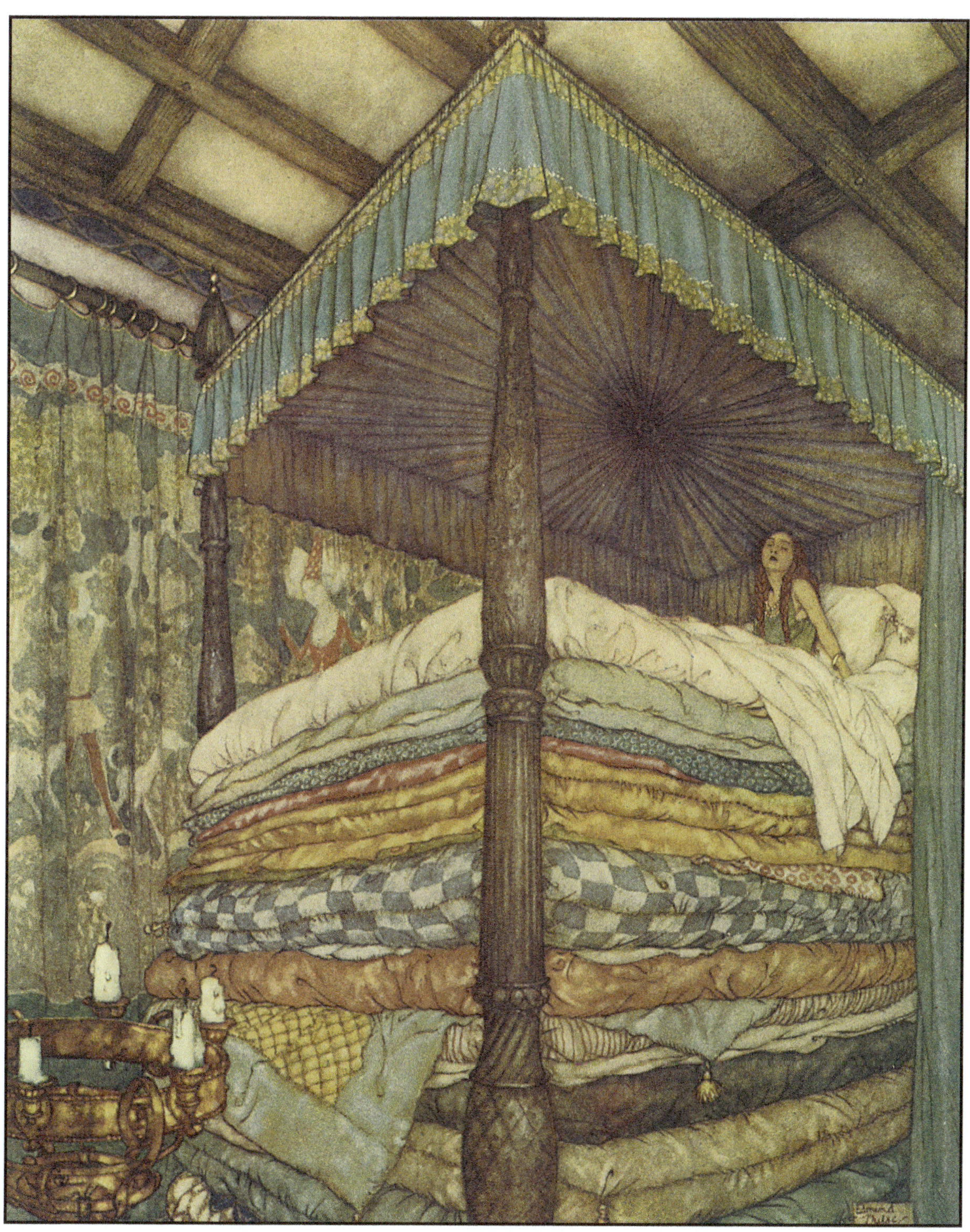

"I have hardly closed my eyes the whole night! Heaven knows what was in my bed. I seemed to be lying upon some hard thing, and my whole body is black and blue this morning. It is terrible!"
From "The Real Princess"

Plate 19

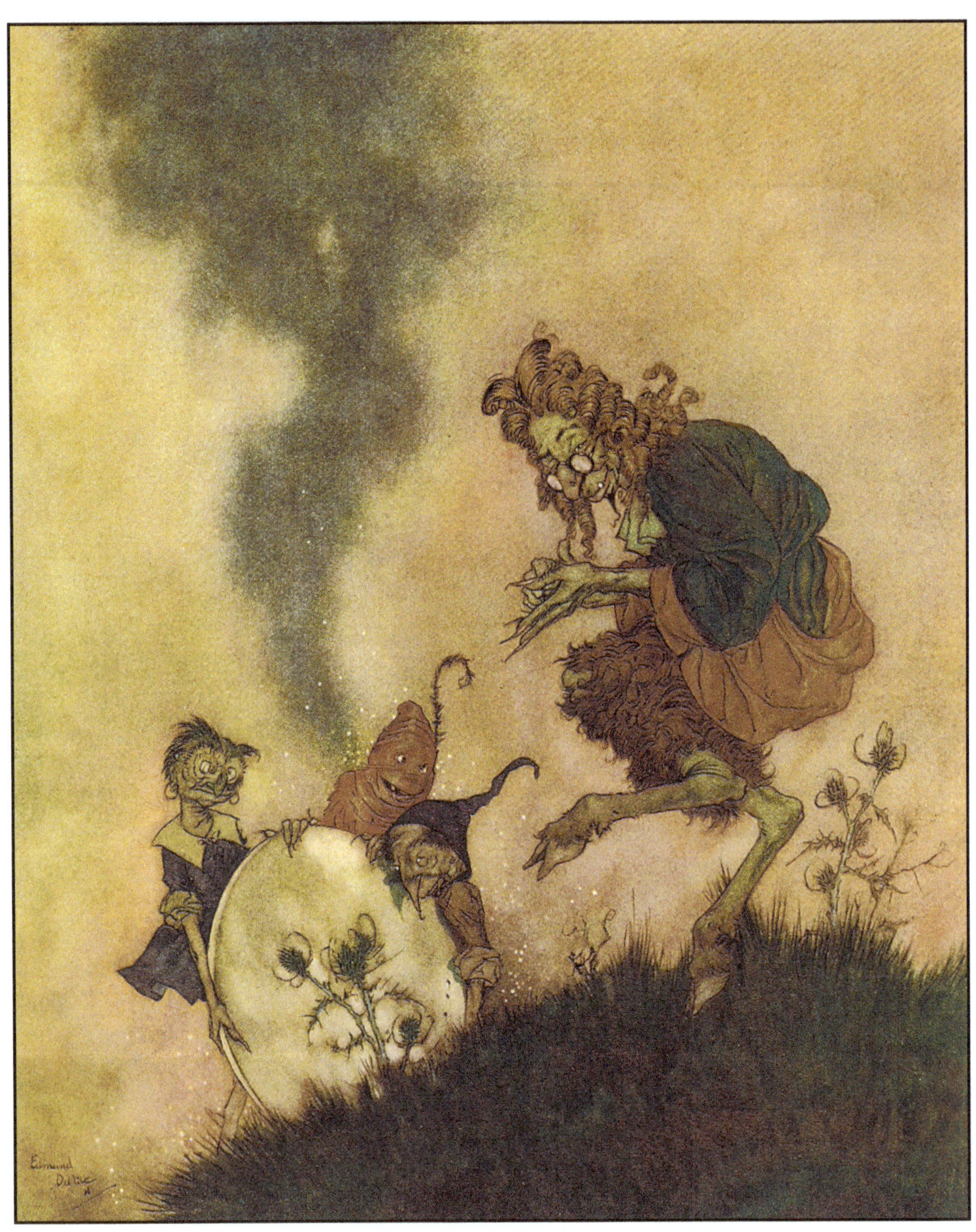

One day he was in a high state of delight because he had invented a mirror with this peculiarity, that every good and pretty thing reflected in it shrank away to almost nothing.
From "The Snow Queen"

Plate 20

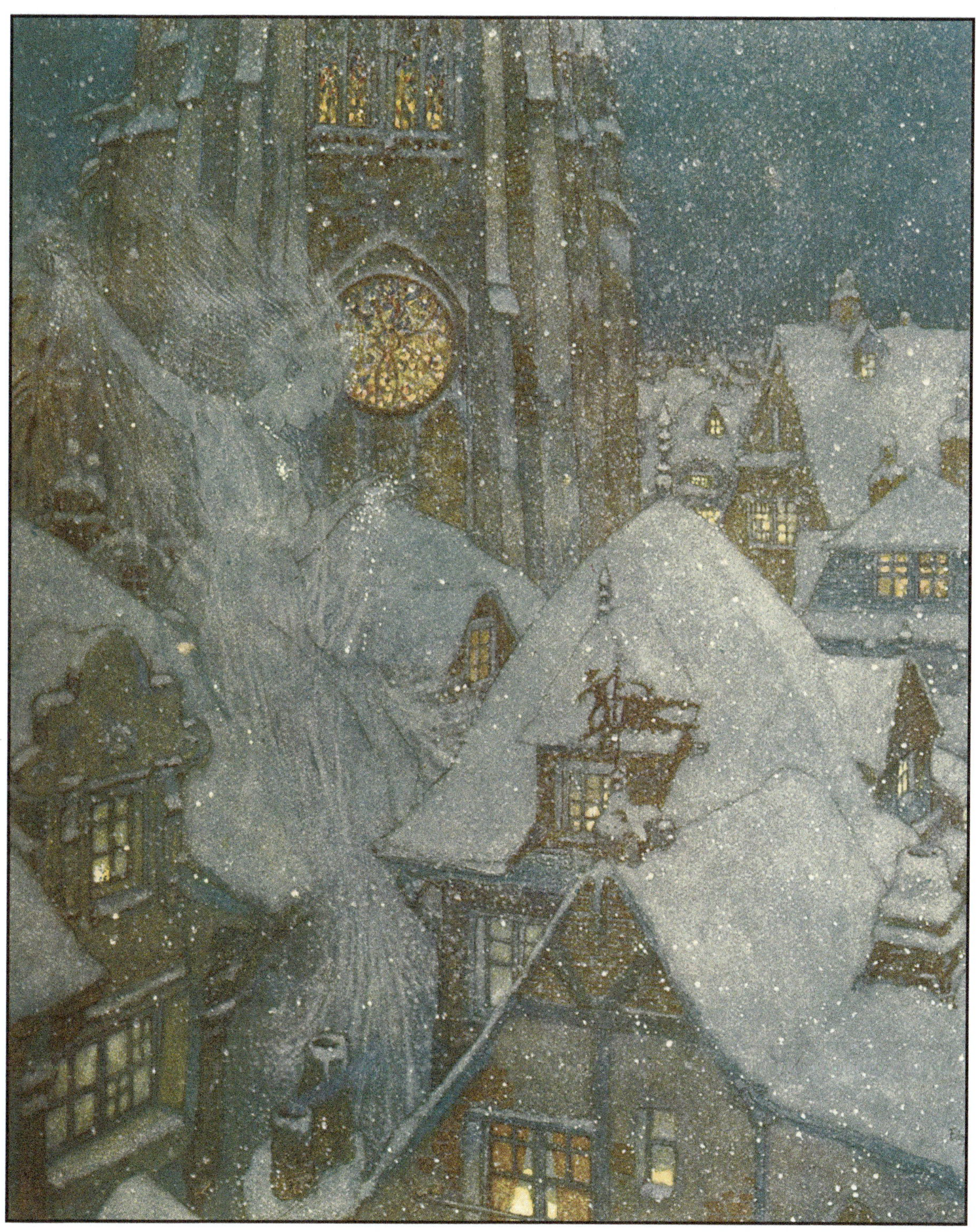

Many a winter's night she flies through the streets and peeps in
at the windows, and then the ice freezes on the panes
into wonderful patterns like flowers.
From "The Snow Queen"

Plate 21

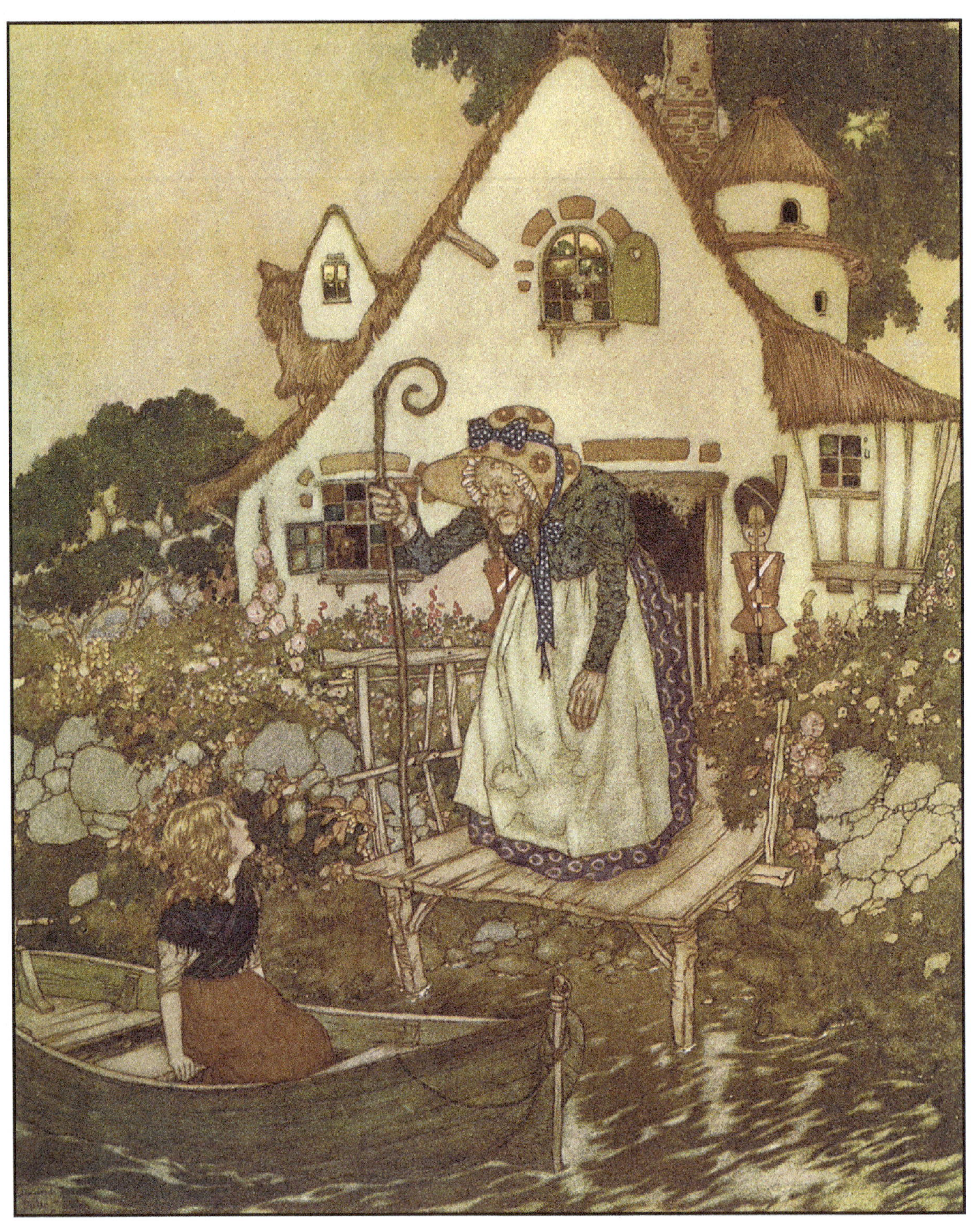

Then an old, old woman came out of the house; she was leaning upon a big, hooked stick, and she wore a big sun hat, which was covered with beautiful painted flowers.
From "The Snow Queen"

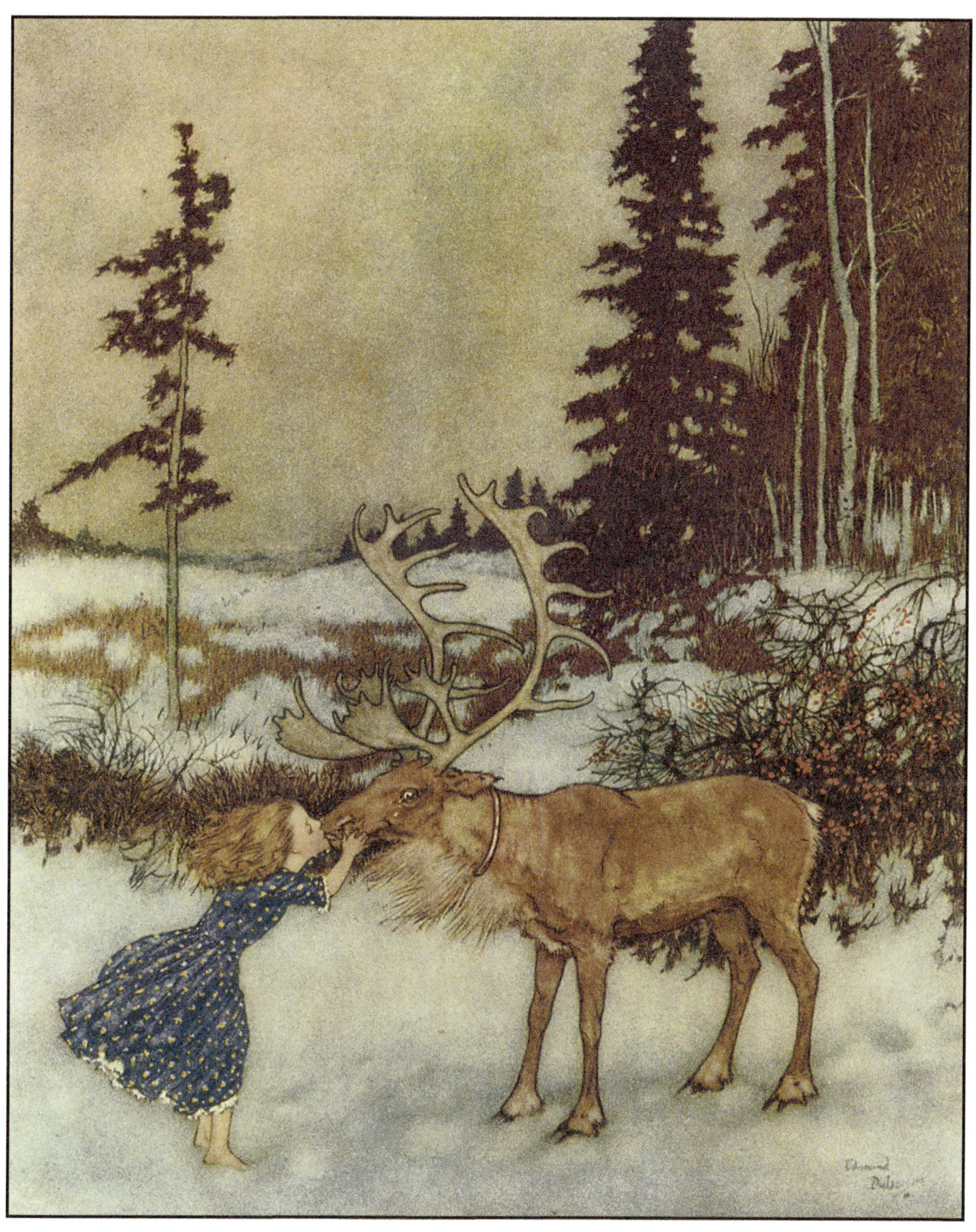

The reindeer did not dare to stop. It ran on till it came to the bush with the red berries. There it put Gerda down, and kissed her on the mouth, while big shining tears trickled down its face.
From "The Snow Queen"

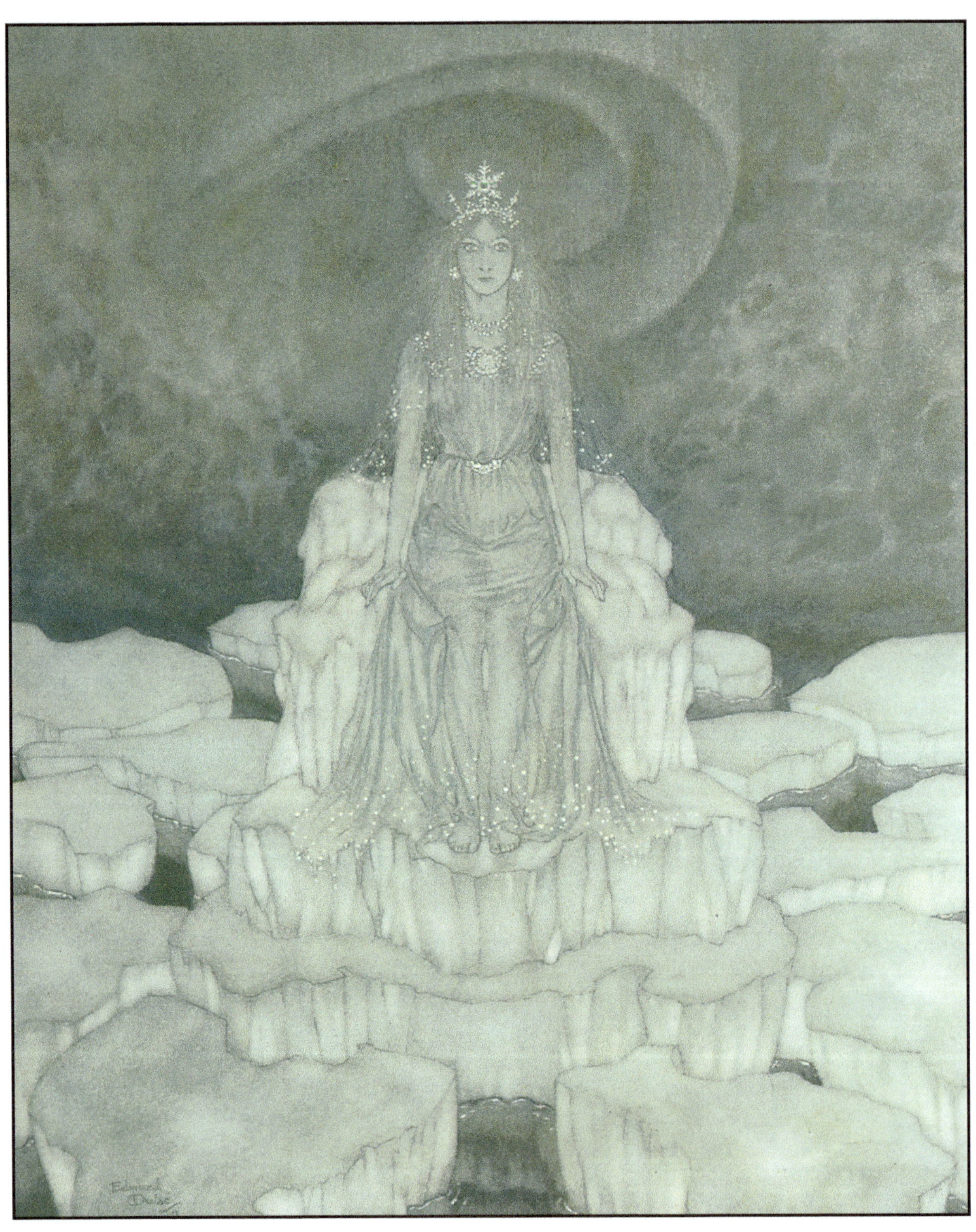

The Snow Queen sat in the very middle of it
when she was at home.
From "The Snow Queen"

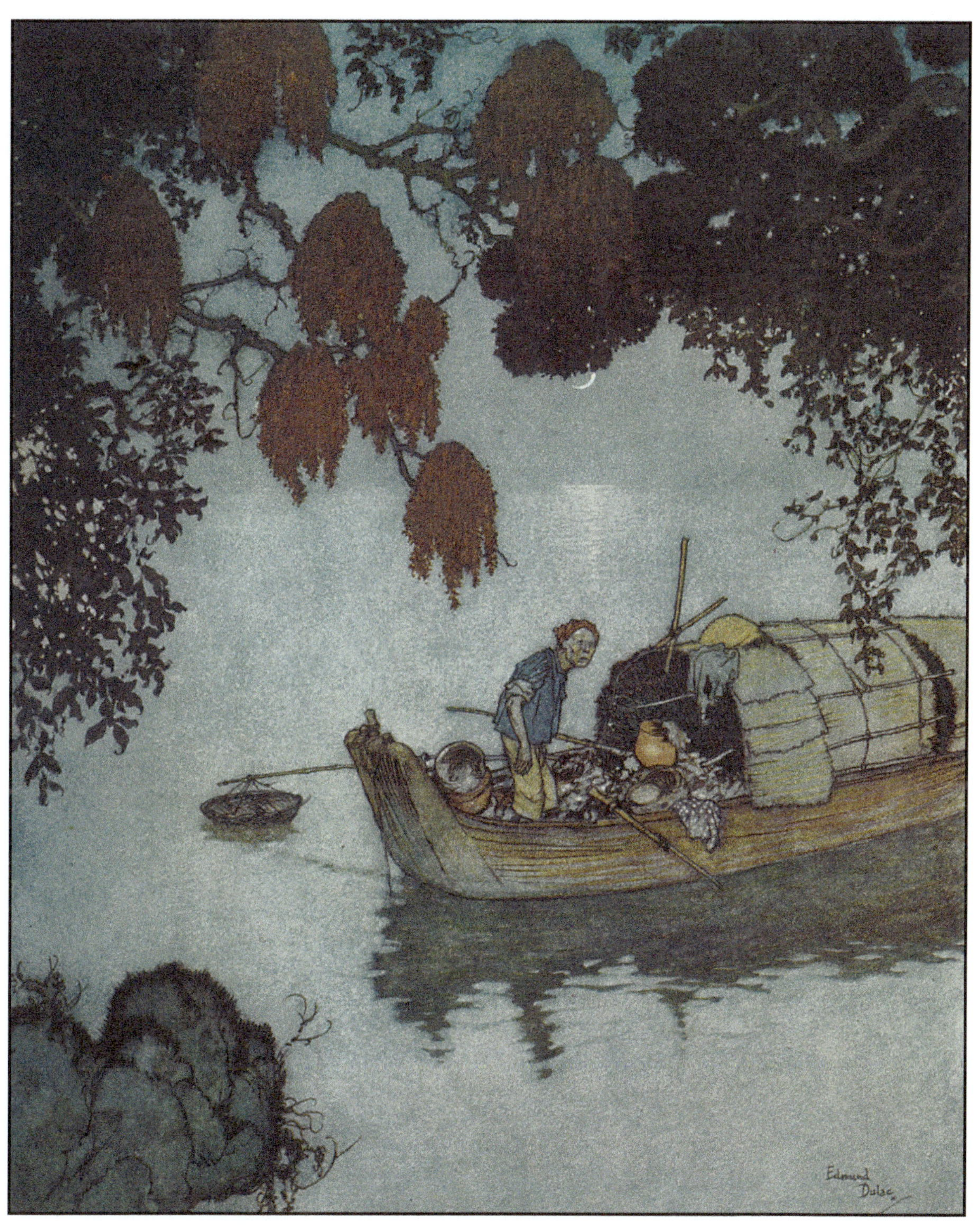

Among these trees lived a nightingale, which sang so deliciously, that even the poor fisherman, who had plenty of other things to do, lay still to listen to it, when he was out at night drawing in his nets.
From "The Nightingale"

Plate 25

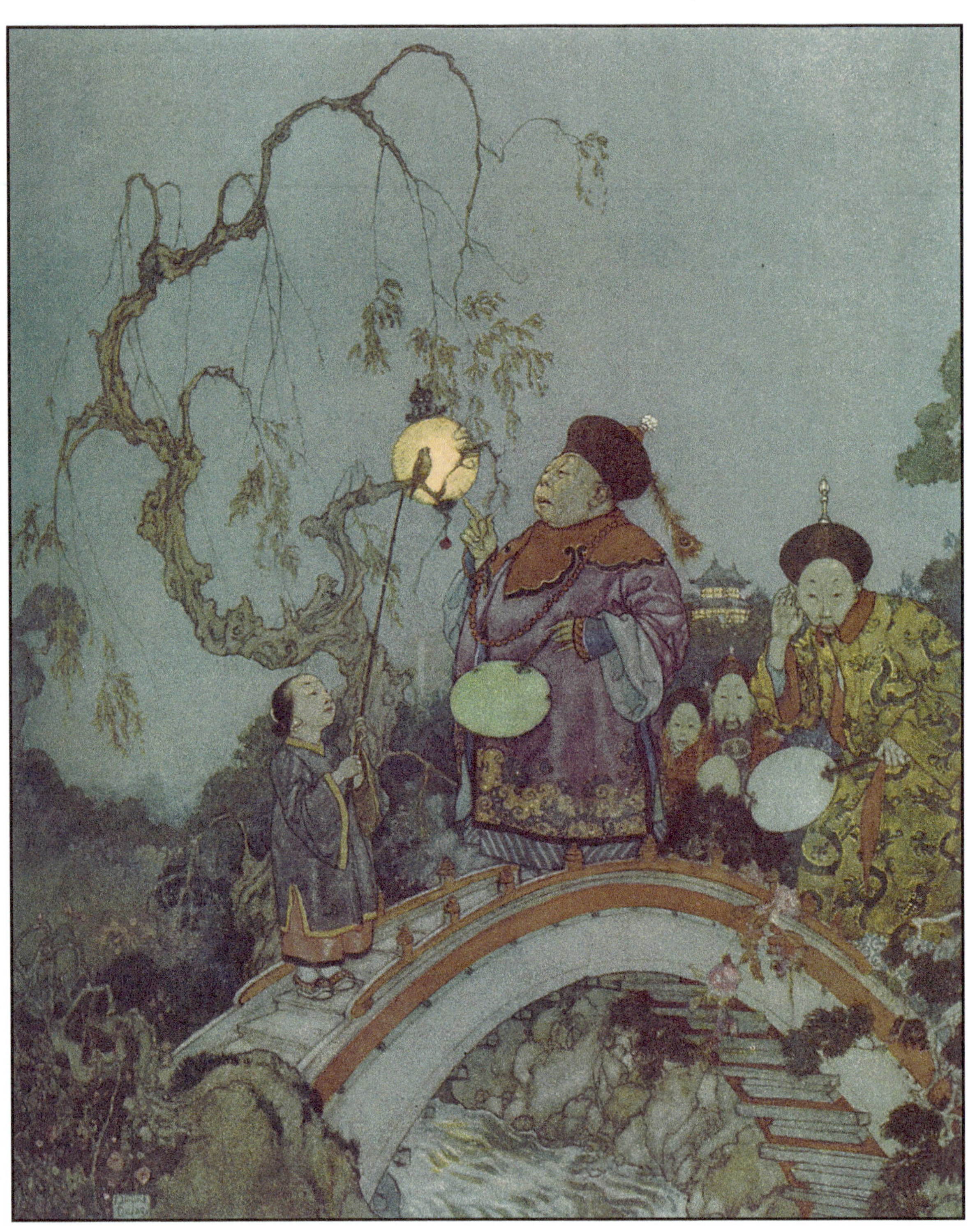

"Is it possible?" said the gentleman-in-waiting.
"I should never have thought it was like that.
How common it looks. Seeing so many grand people
must have frightened all its colors away."
From "The Nightingale"

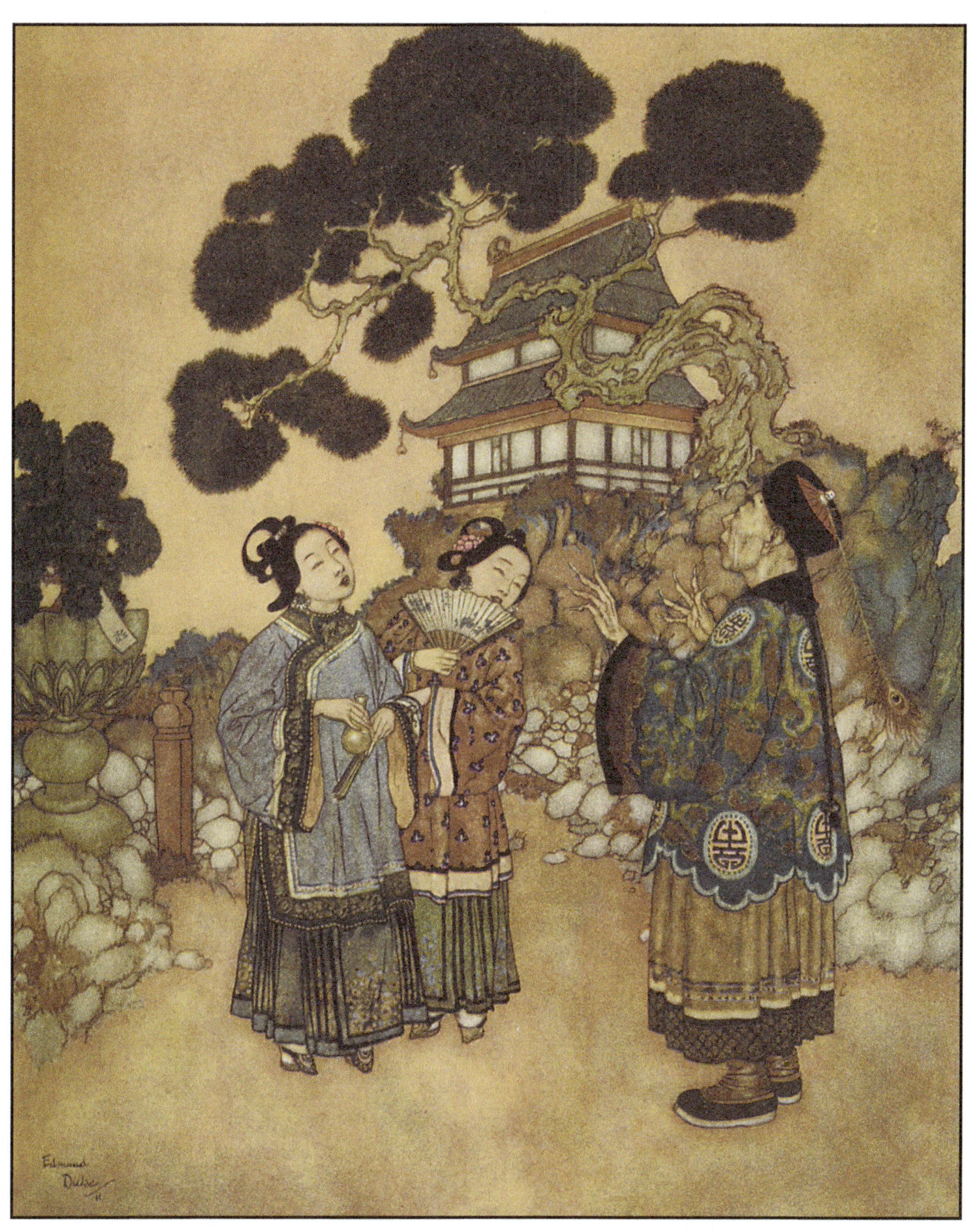

Then it again burst into its sweet heavenly song. "That is the most delightful coquetting I have ever seen!" said the ladies, and they took some water into their mouths to try and make the same gurgling, thinking so to equal the nightingale.
From "The Nightingale"

Plate 27

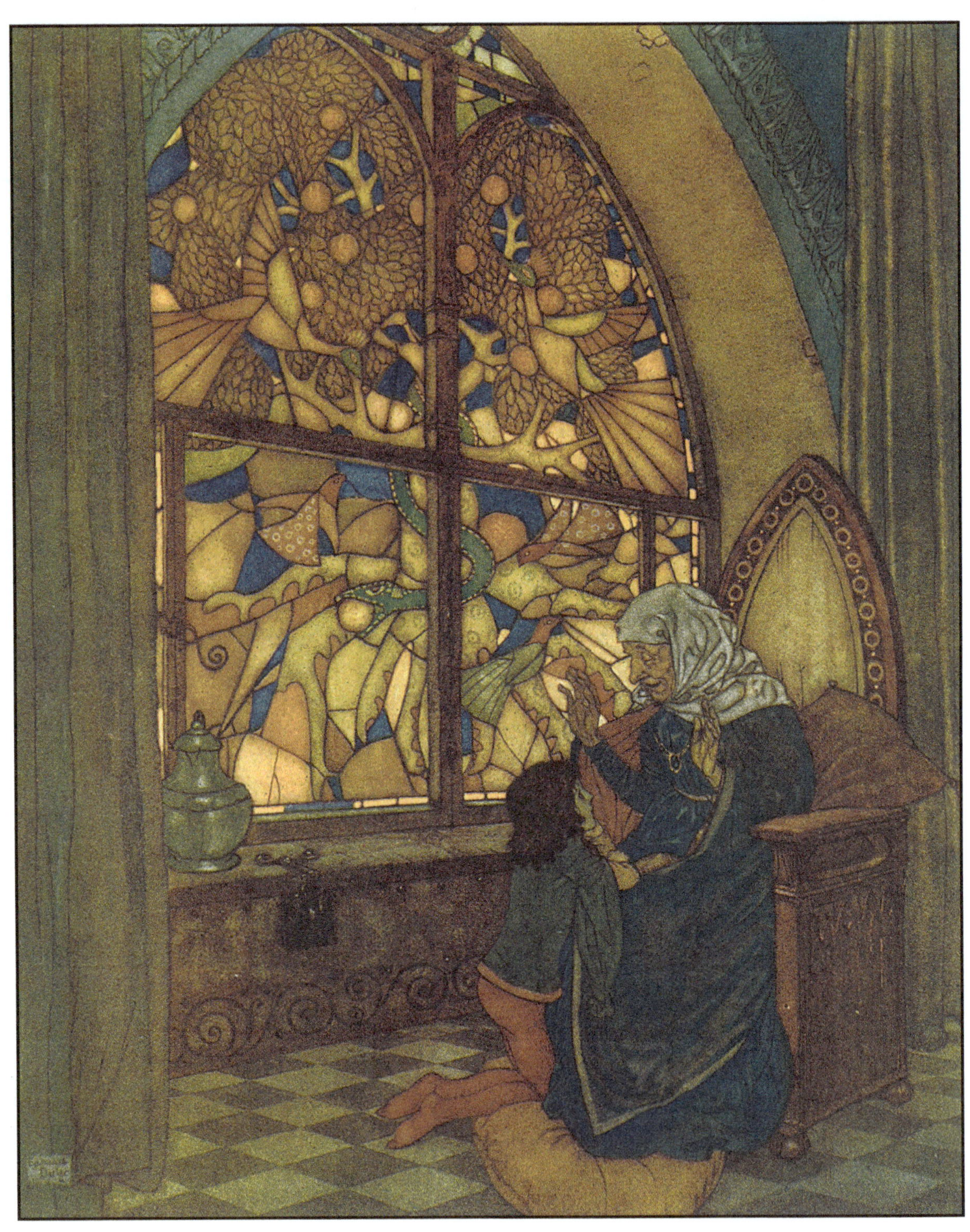

His grandmother had told him, when he was quite a little fellow
and was about to begin his school life, that every flower
in the Garden of Paradise was a delicious cake
and that the pistils were full of wine.
From "The Garden of Paradise"

Plate 28

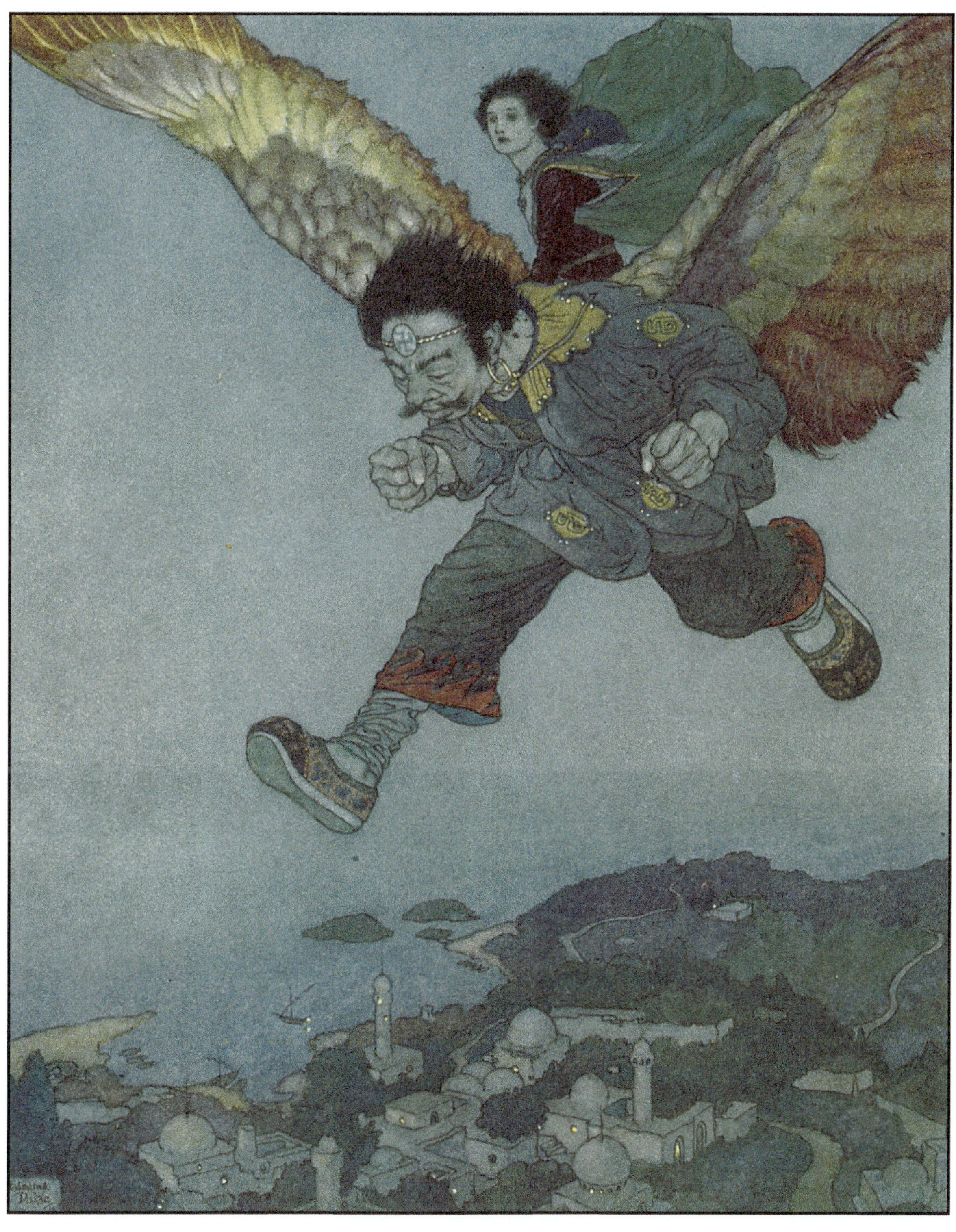

The eagle in the great forest flew swiftly,
but the Eastwing flew more swiftly still.
From "The Garden of Paradise"

Plate 29

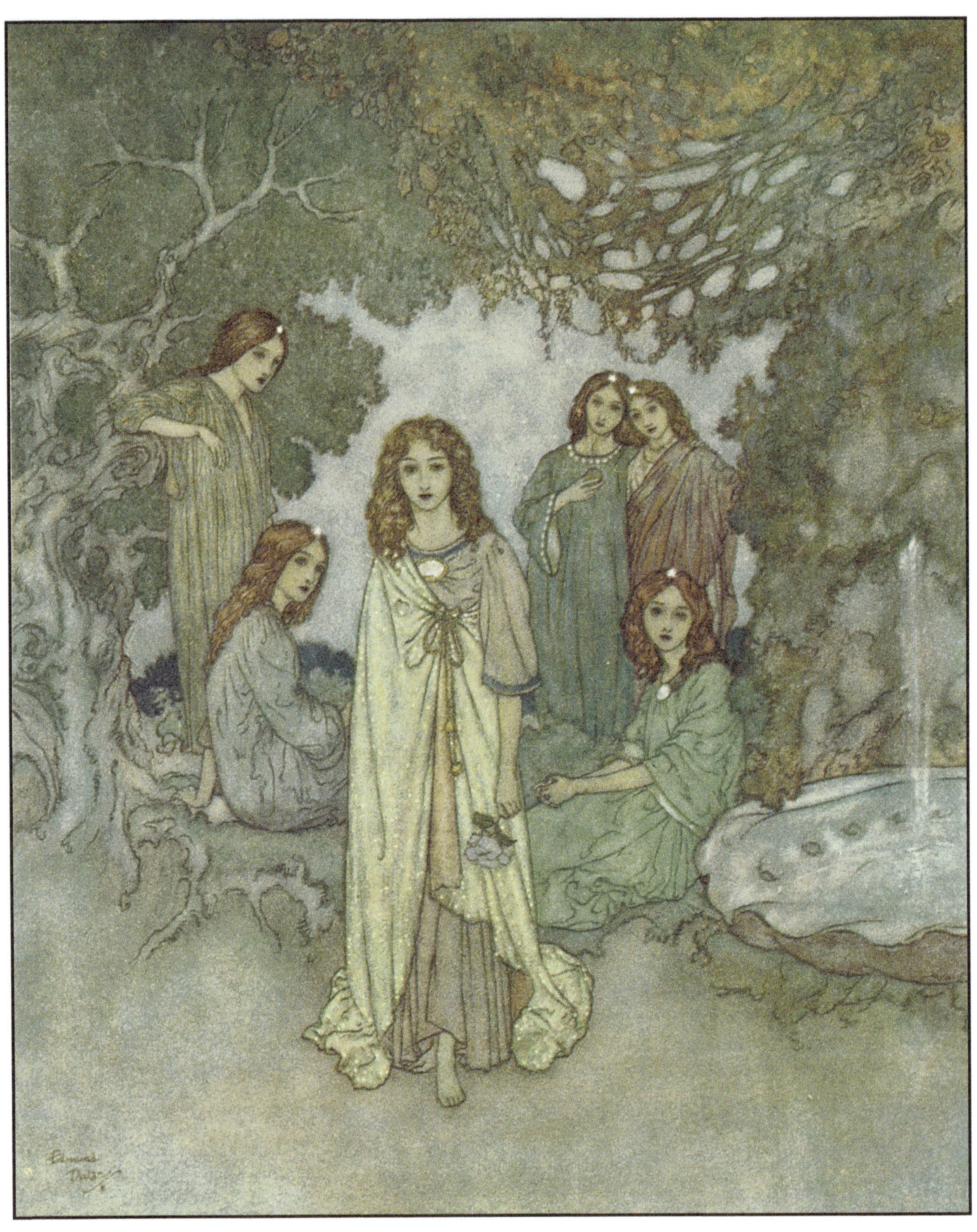

The Fairy of the Garden now advanced to meet them; her garments shone like the sun, and her face beamed like that of a happy mother rejoicing over her child.
From "The Garden of Paradise"

Plate 30

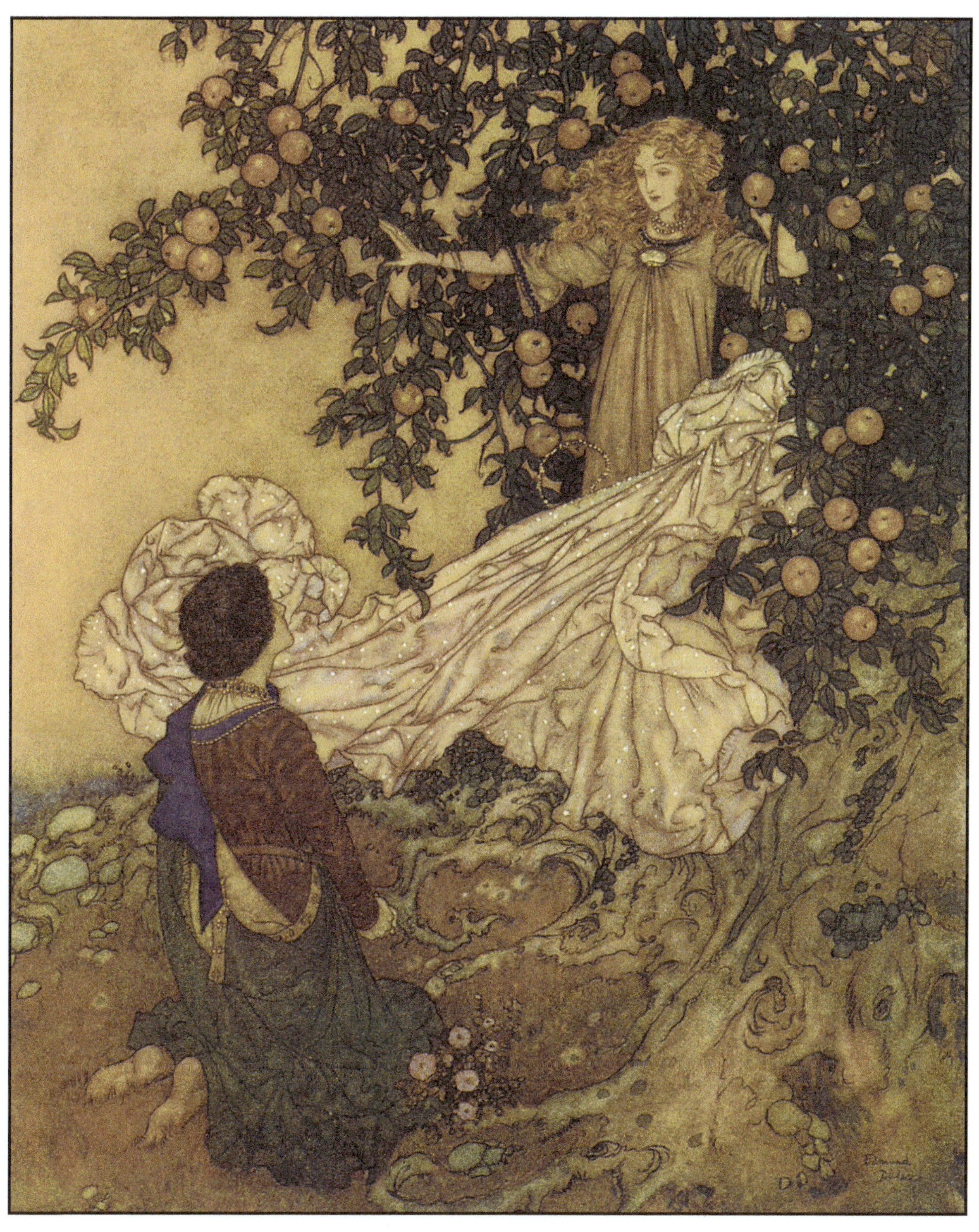

The Fairy dropped her shimmering garment, drew back the branches, and a moment after was hidden within their depths.
From "The Garden of Paradise"

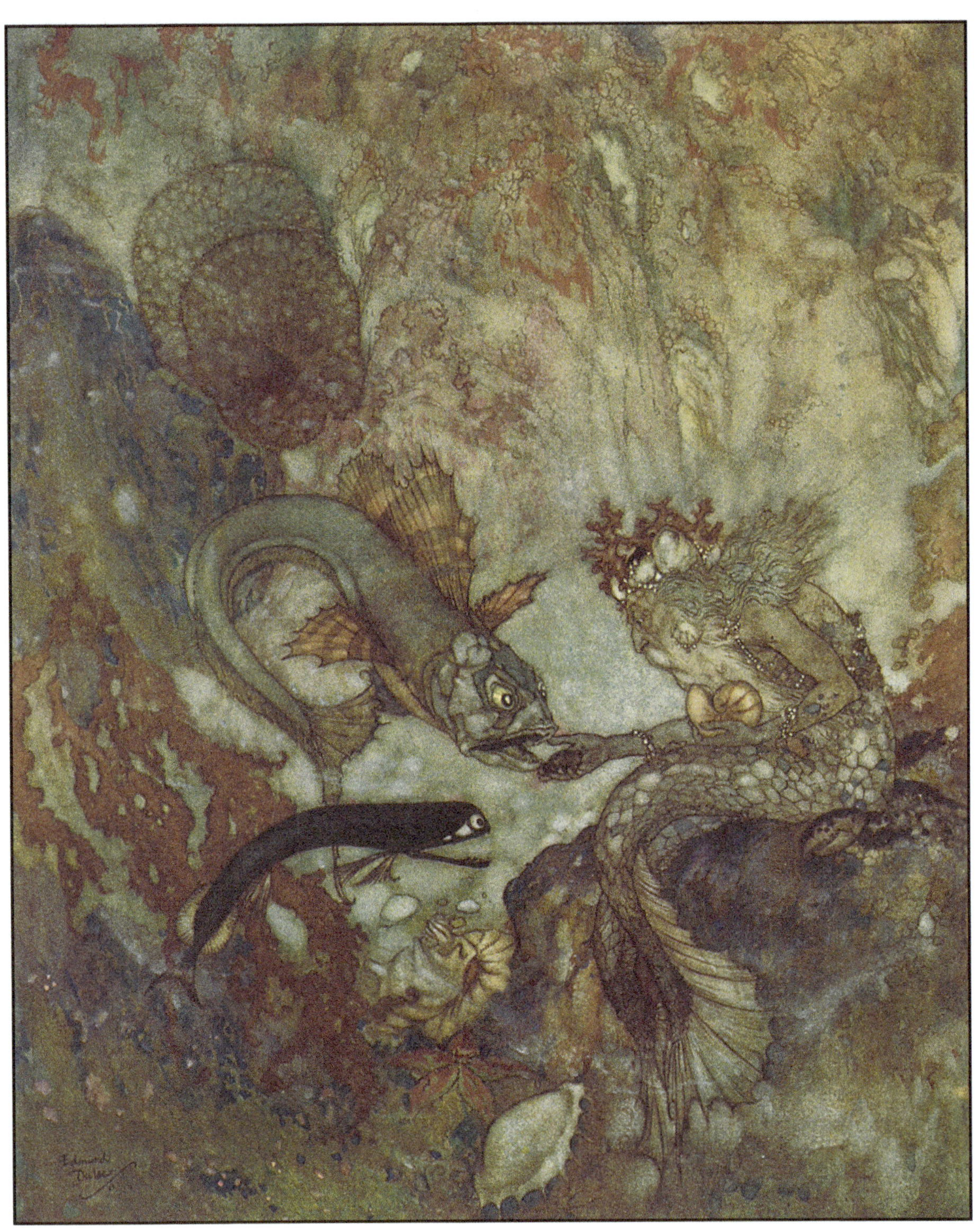

The Merman King had been for many years a widower, but his old mother kept house for him; she was a clever woman, but so proud of her noble birth that she wore twelve oysters on her tail, while other grandees were only allowed six.
From "The Mermaid"

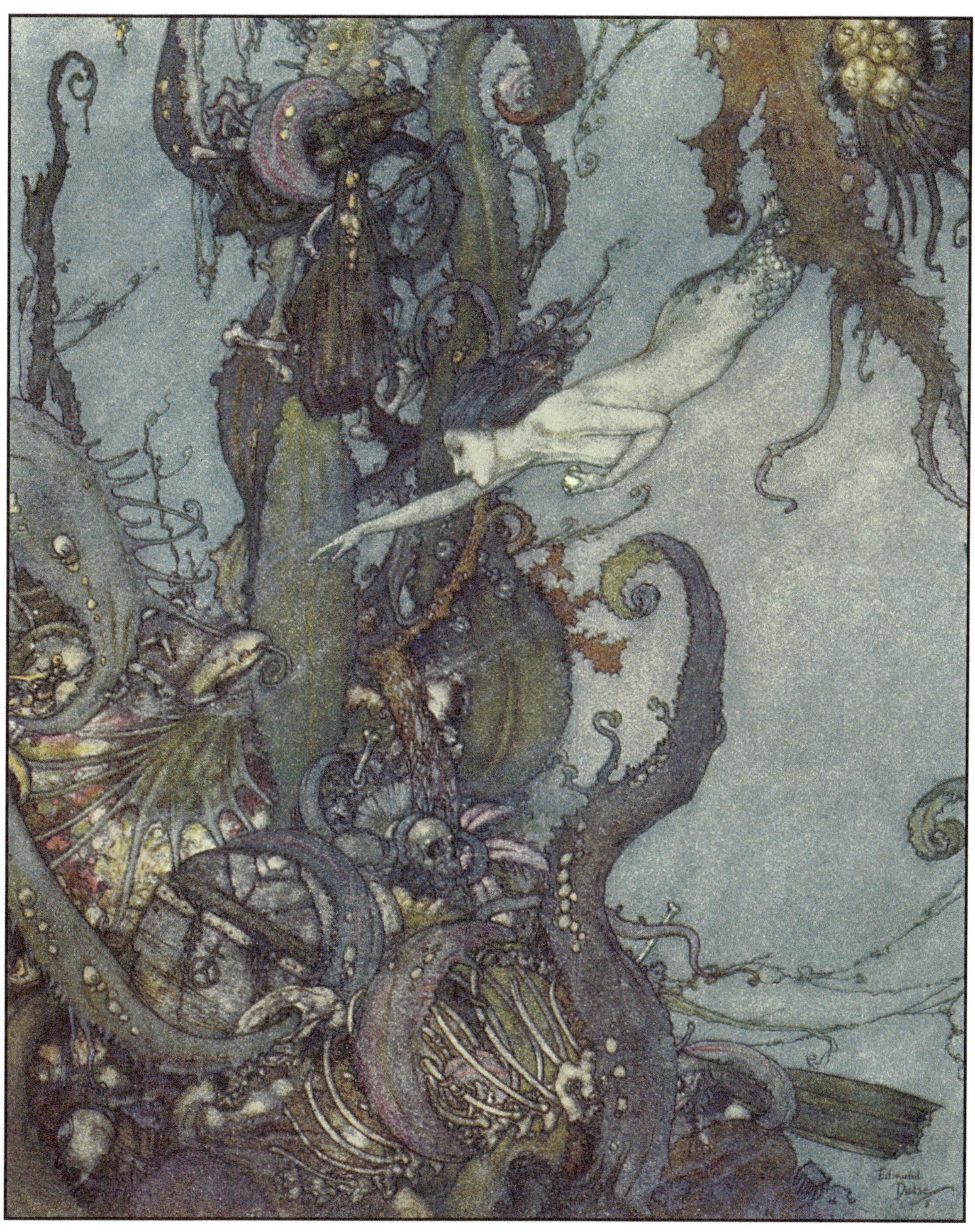

But the little mermaid had no need to do this, for at the mere sight of the bright liquid which sparkled in her hand like a shining star, they drew back in terror.
From "The Mermaid"

Plate 33

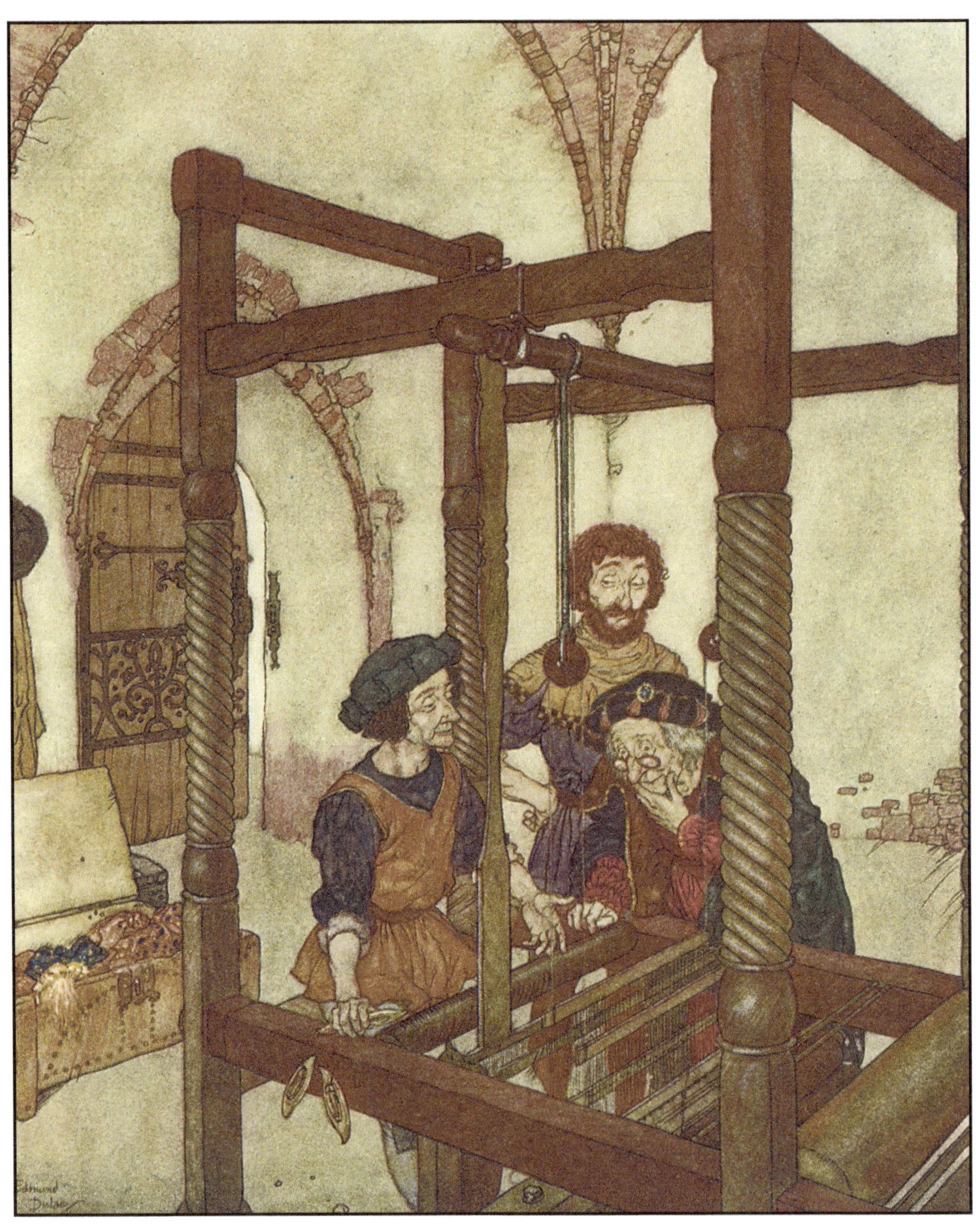

They pointed to the empty loom, and the poor old minister stared as hard as he could, but he could not see anything, for of course there was nothing to see.
From "The Emperor's New Clothes"

Plate 34

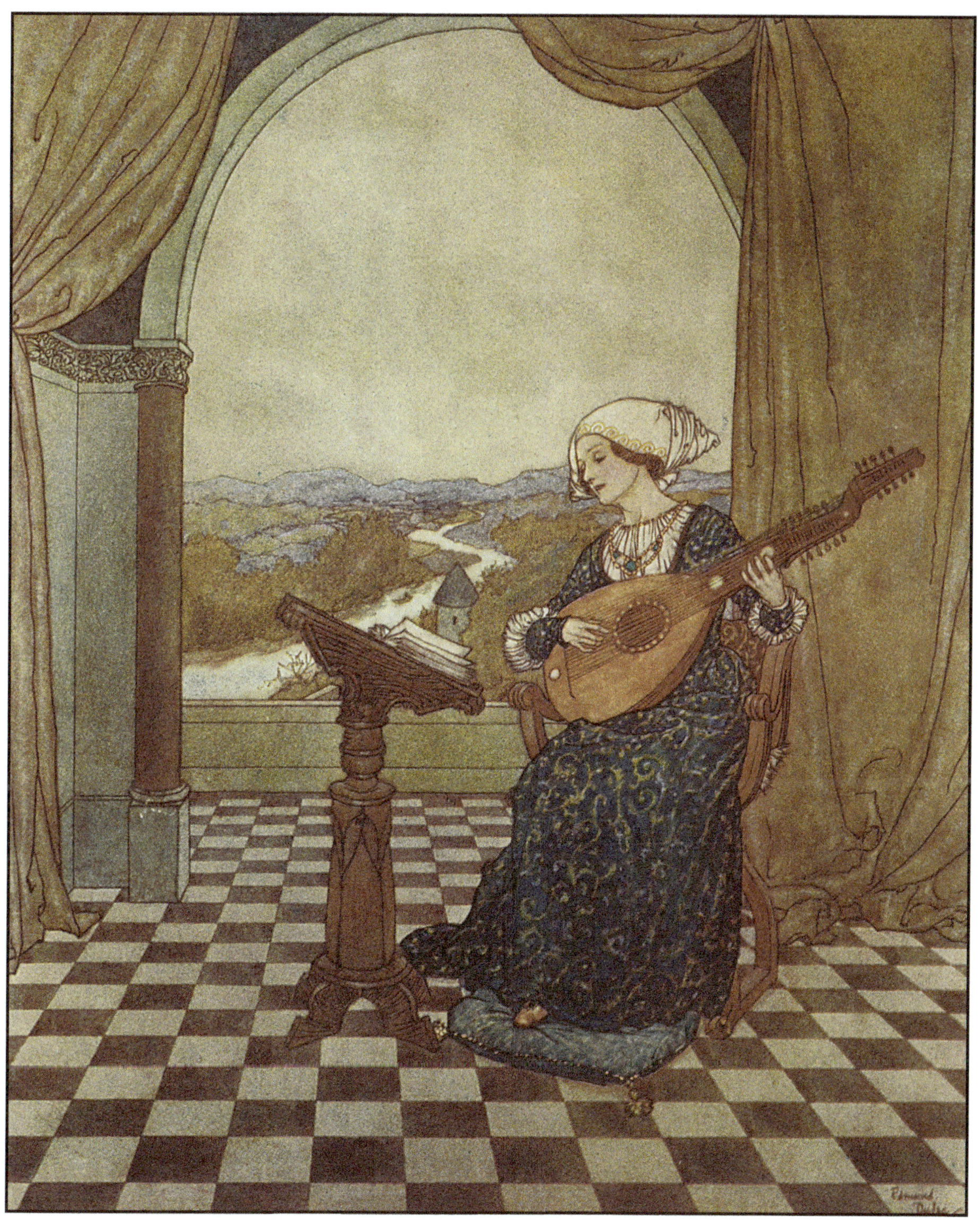

She played upon the ringing lute, and sang to its tones.
From "The Wind's Tale"

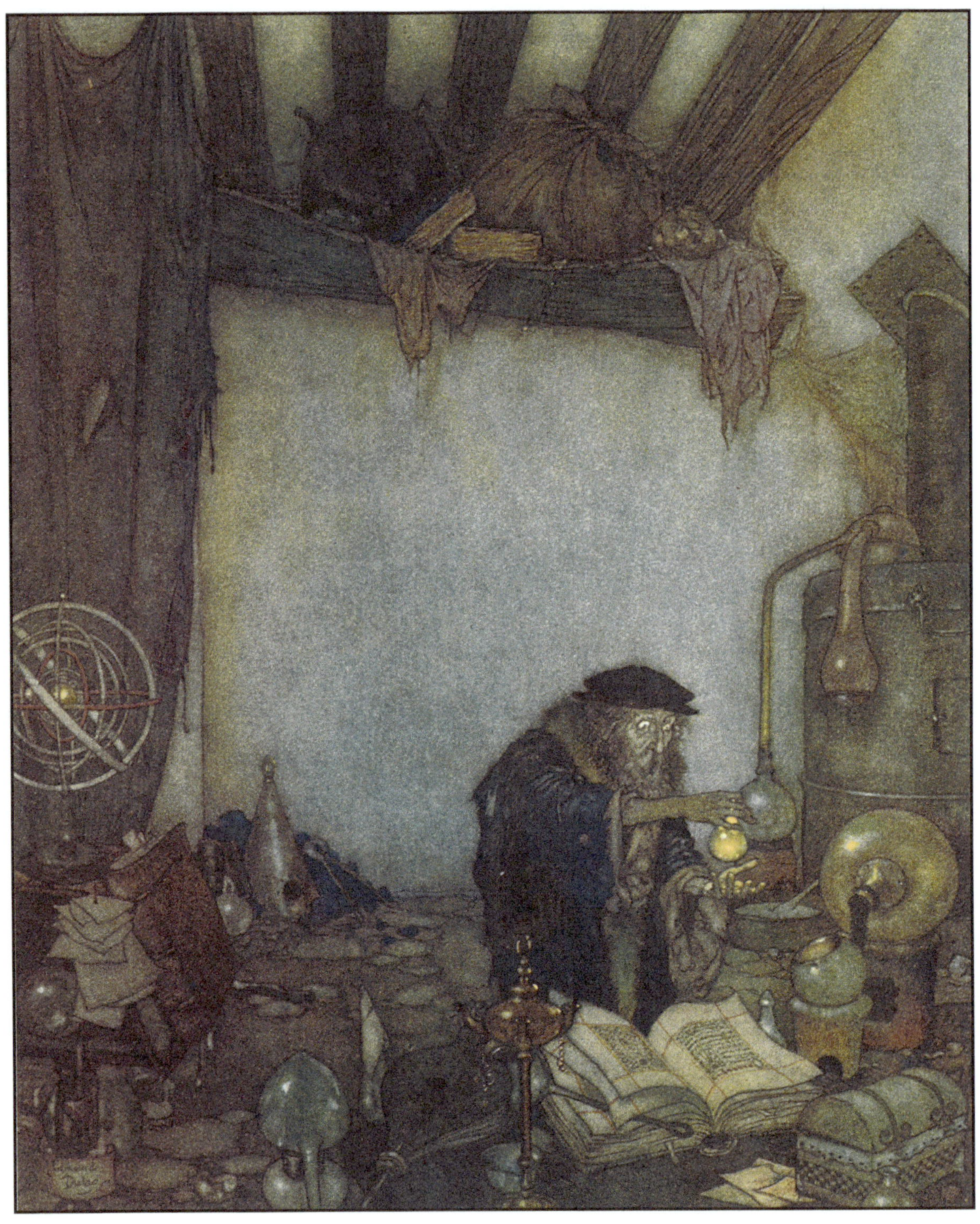

He lifted it with a trembling hand and shouted with a trembling voice: "Gold! gold!"
From "The Wind's Tale"

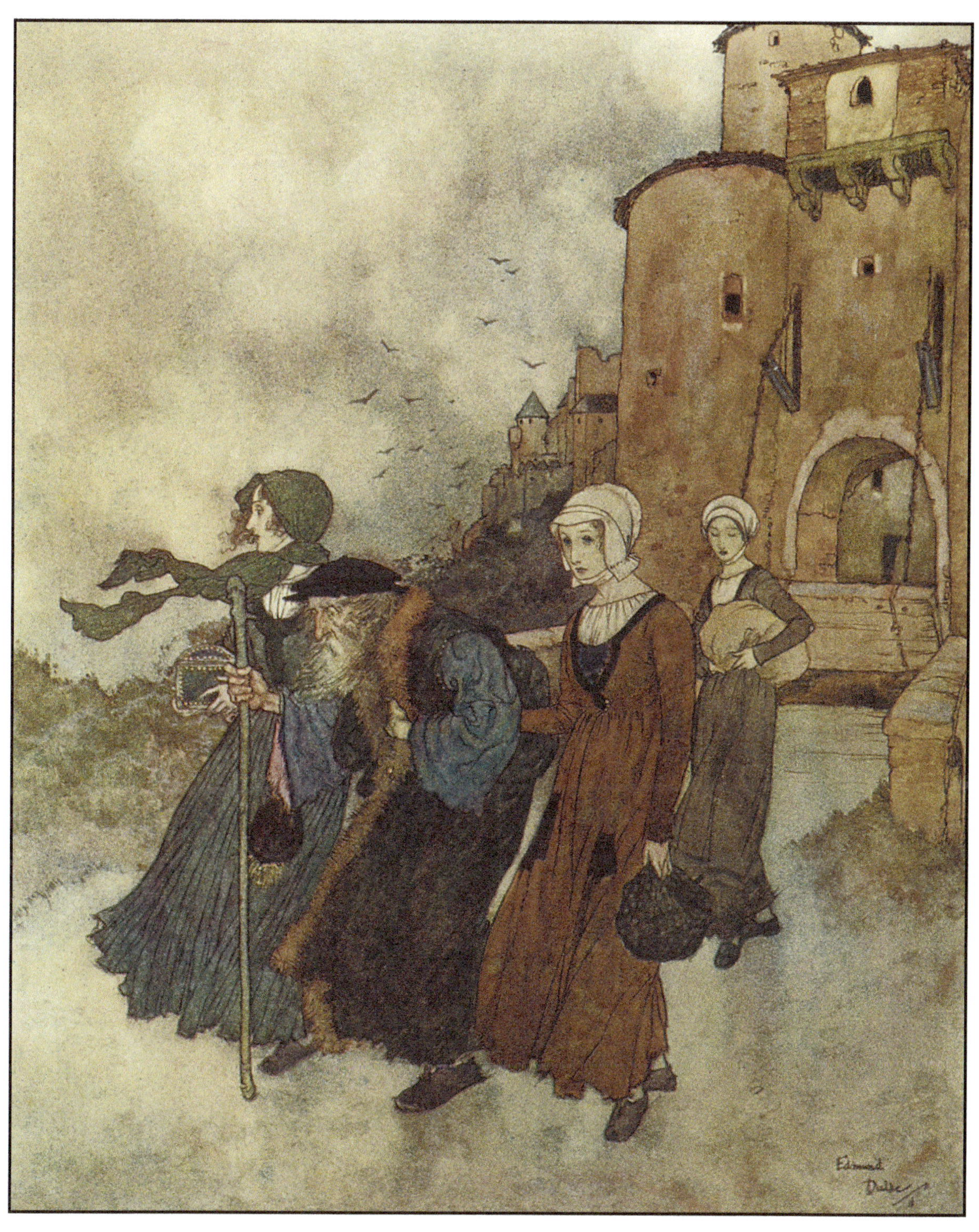

Waldemar Daa had it in his bosom, took his staff in his hand, and, with his three daughters, the once wealthiest gentleman walked out of Borreby Hall for the last time.
From "The Wind's Tale"

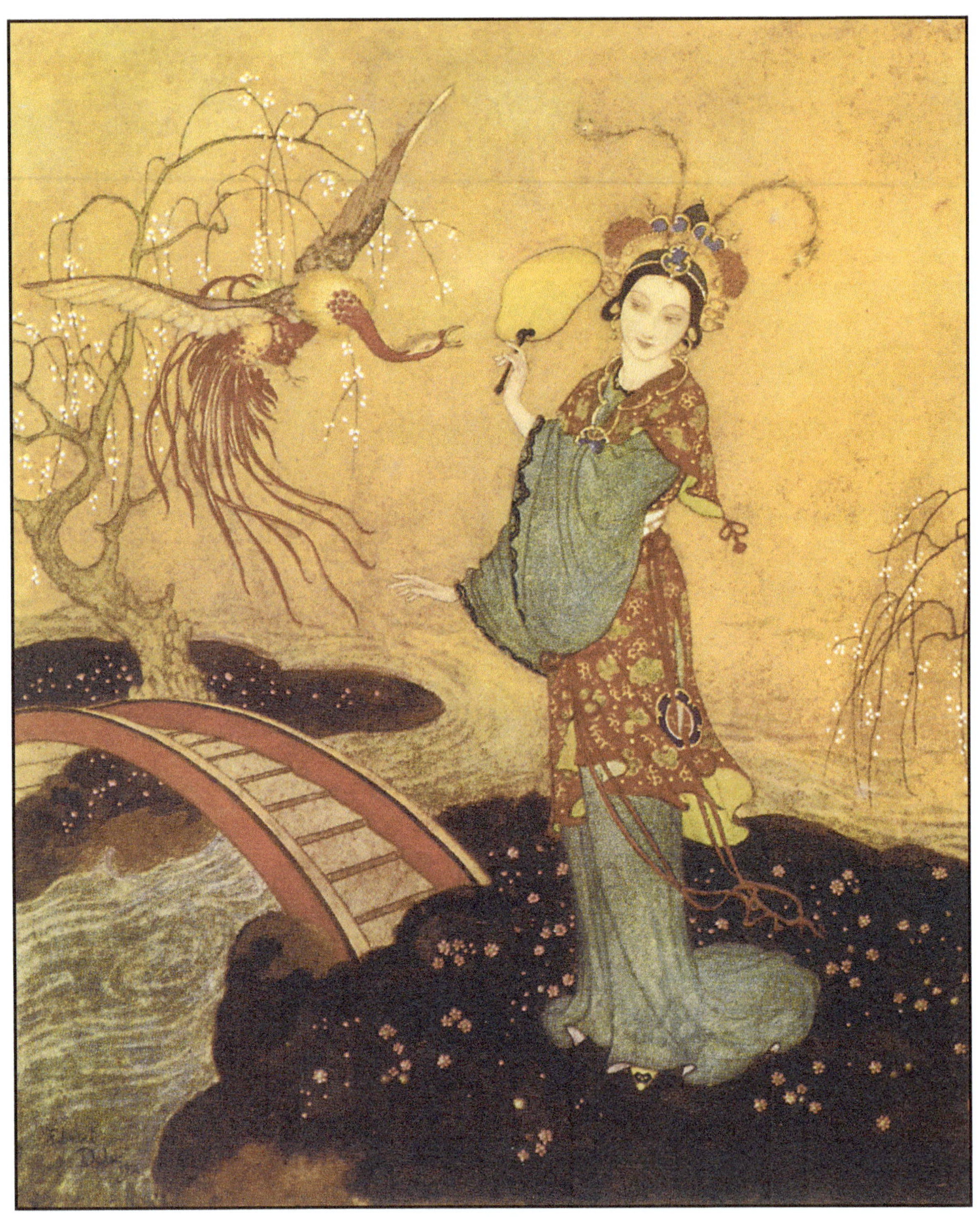

Princess Badoura
From "Princess Badoura"

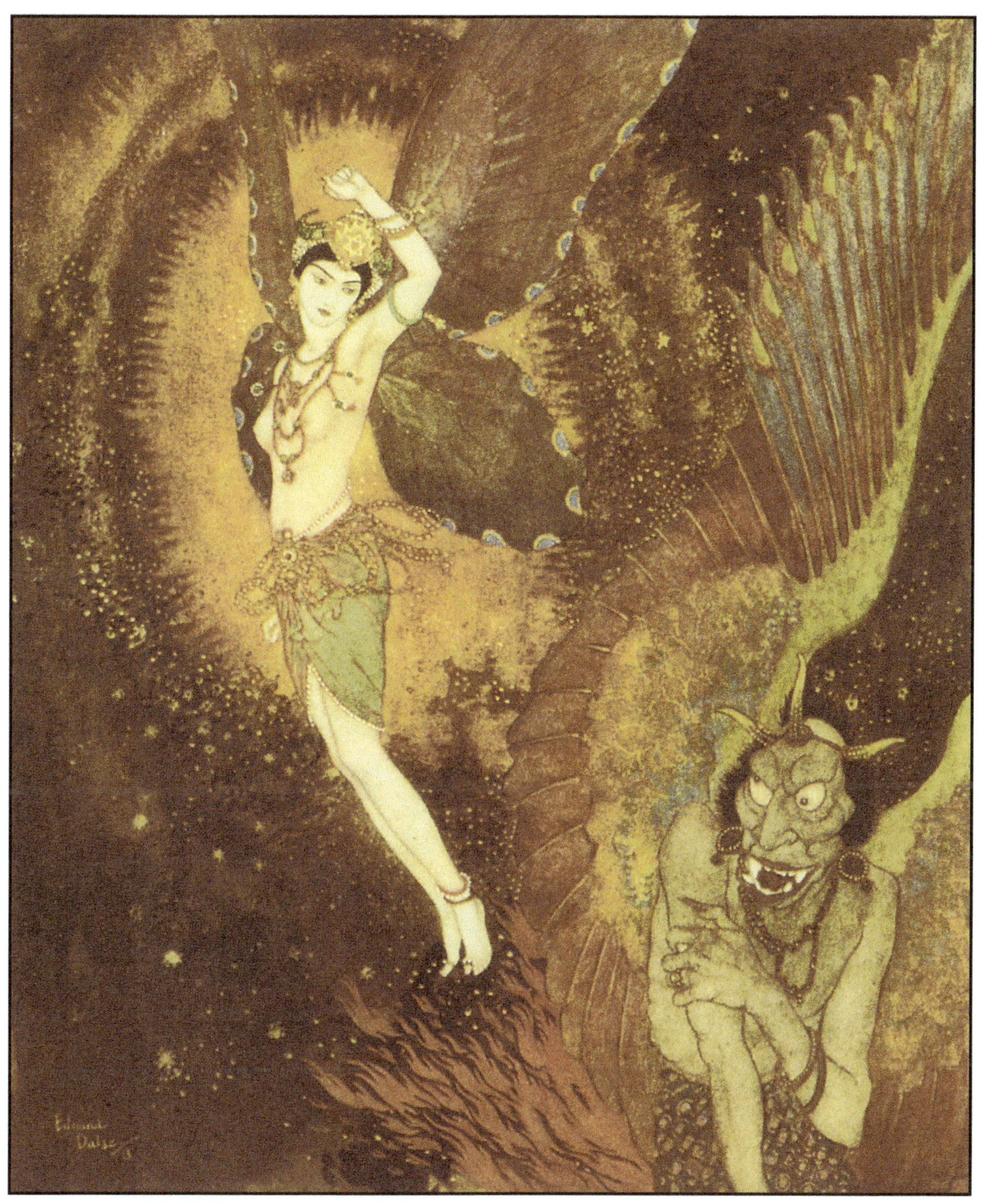

As she rose up through the clouds there passed one she knew by his name to be Dahnash.
From "The History of Badoura, Princess of China, and of Camaralzaman, The Island Prince"

Plate 39

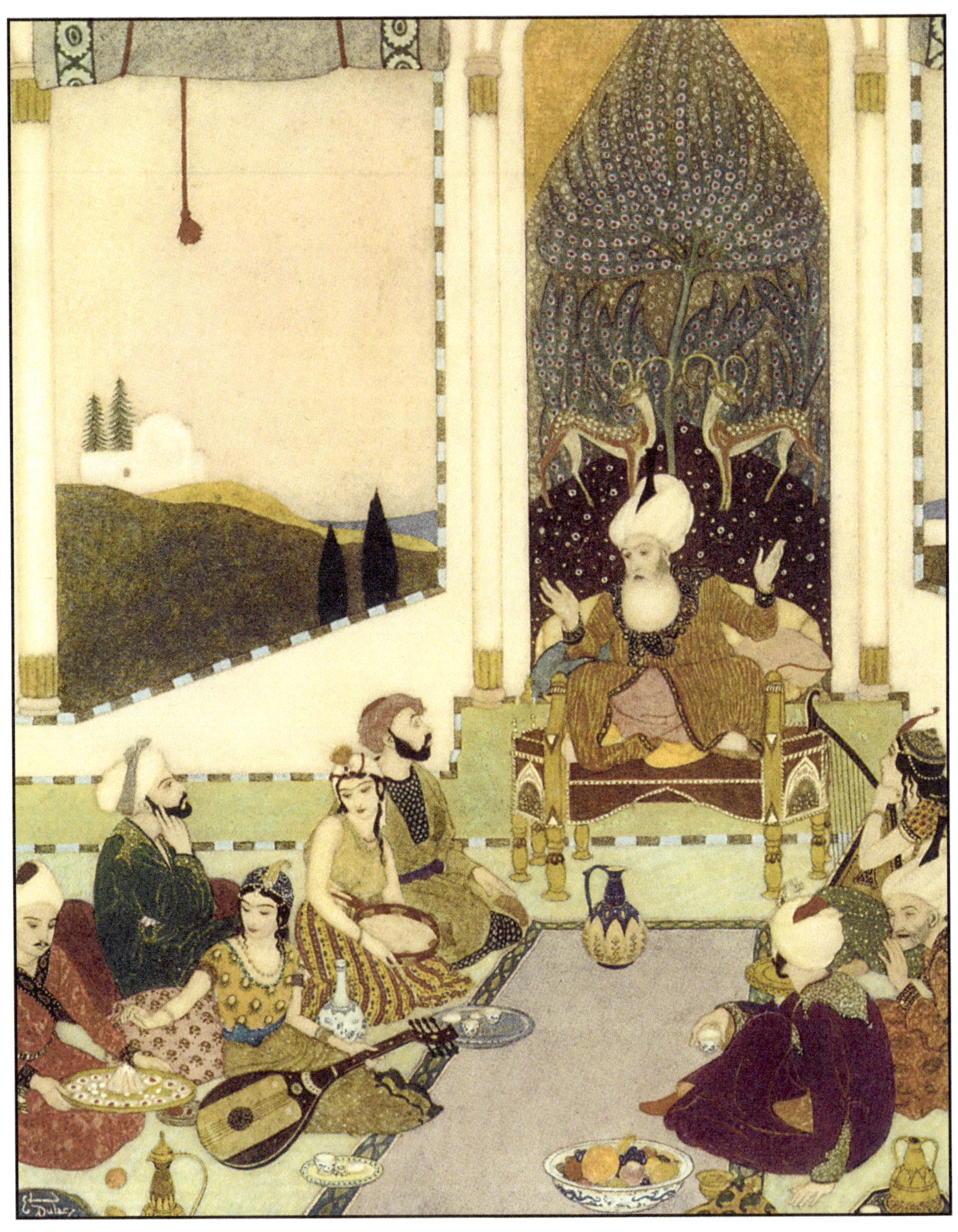

Sindbad the Sailor entertains Sindbad the Landsman.
Frontispiece from
"Sindbad the Sailor and Other Stories from the Arabian Nights"

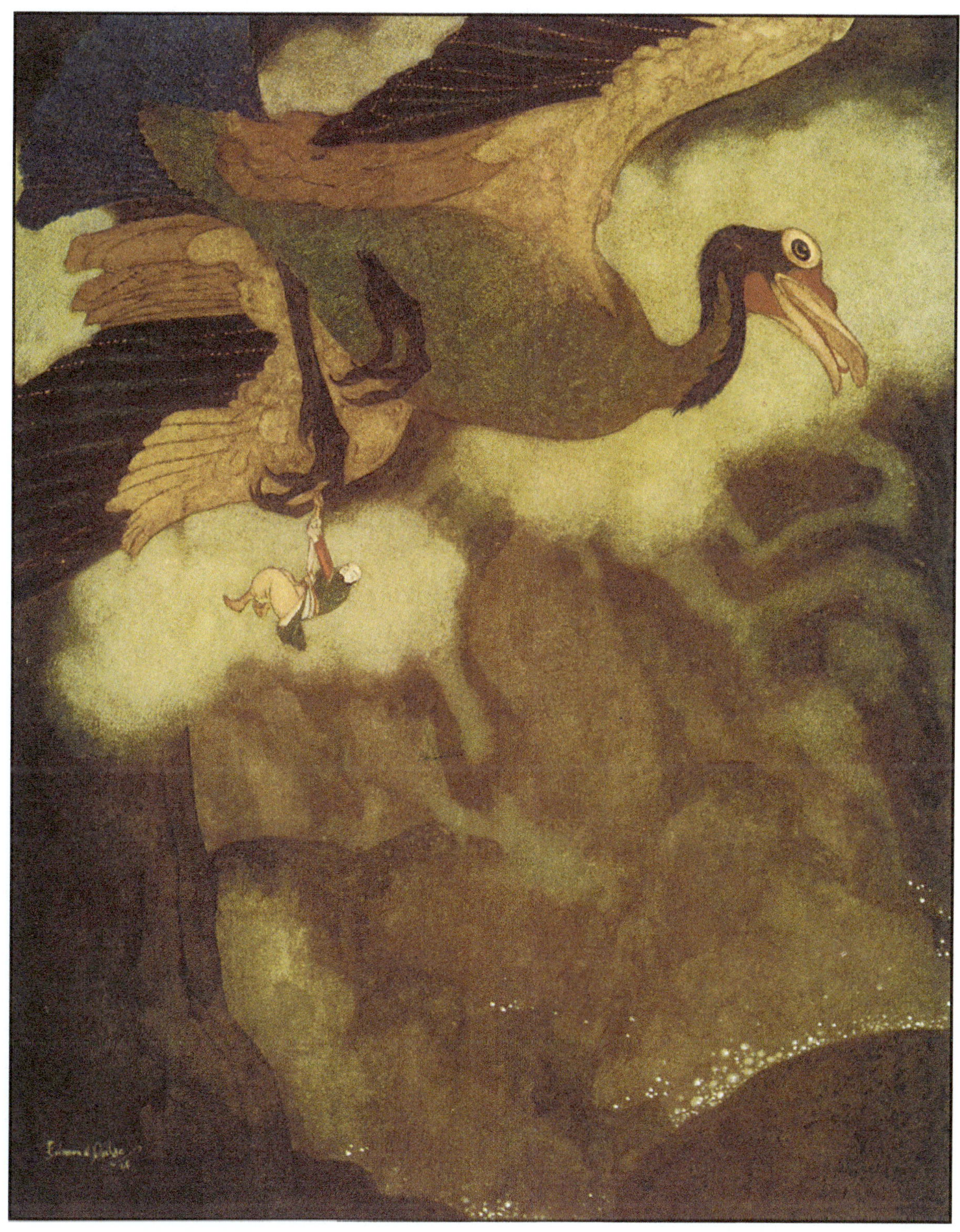

The Episode of the Rokh
From "Sindbad the Sailor"

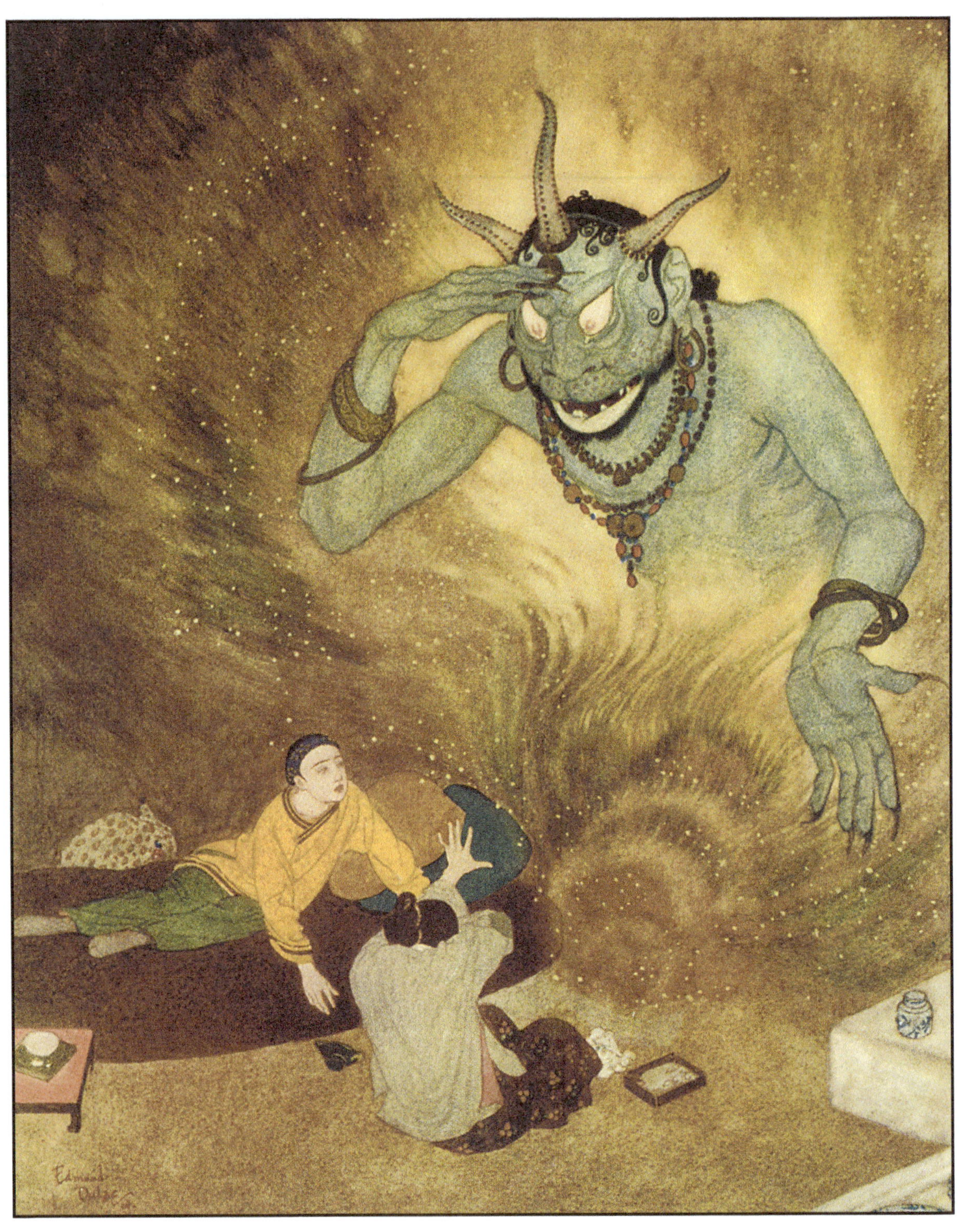

Aladdin and the Efrite.
From "Aladdin and the Wonderful Lamp"

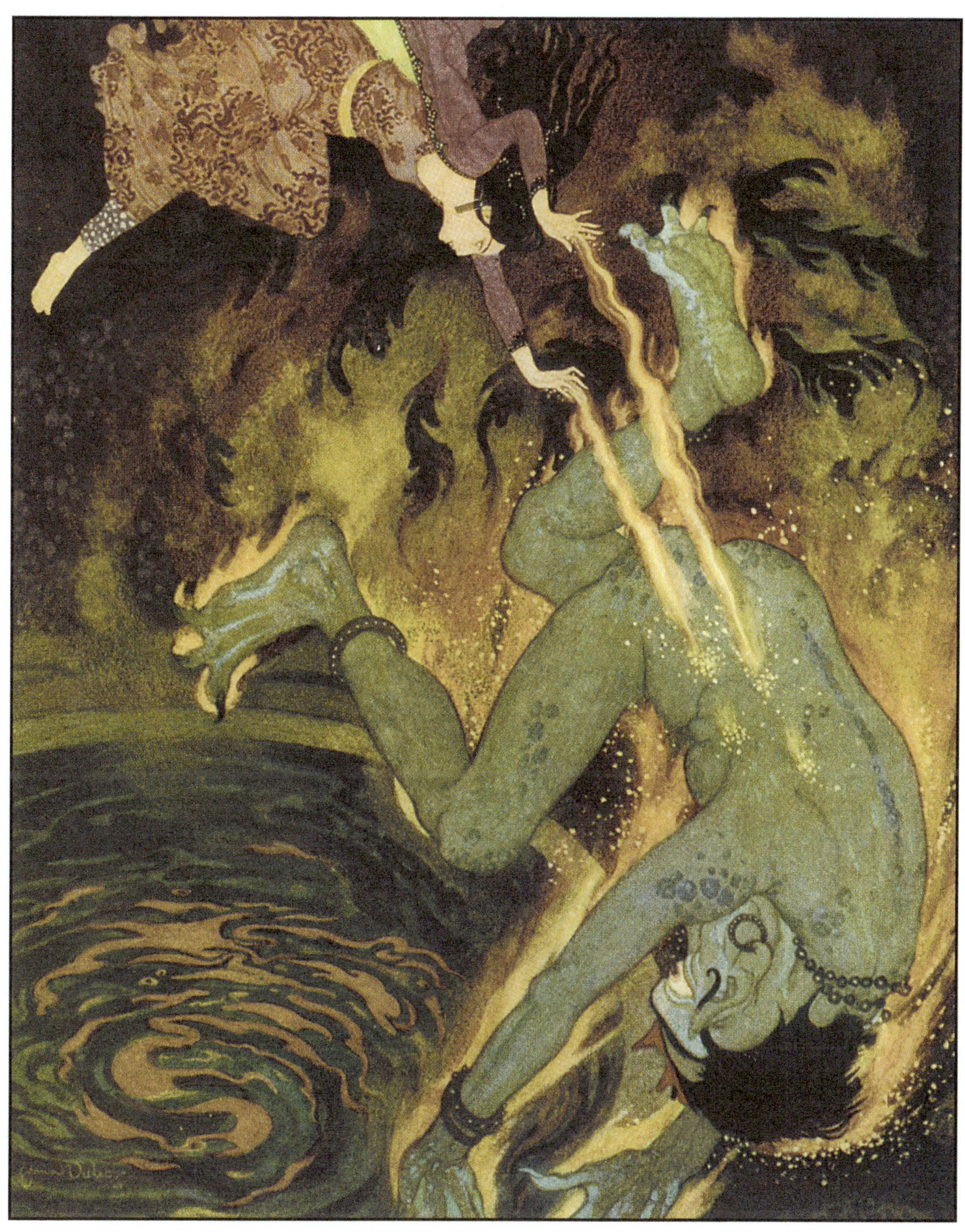

The Princess burns the Efrite to death.
From "The Story of the Three Calendars"

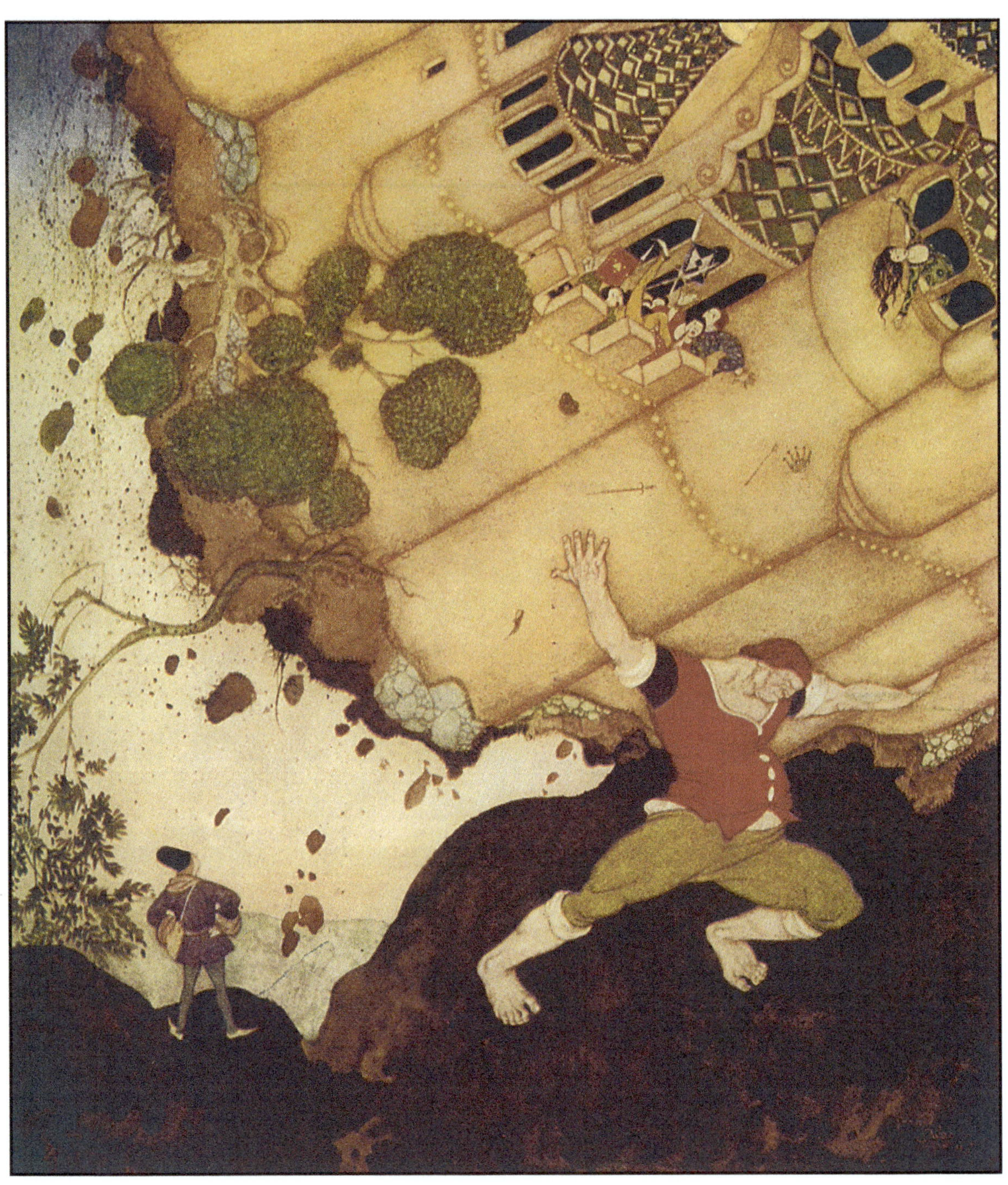

"Hi! friend! Take the whole castle, with the Queen and all it contains, on your shoulders!"
From "The Seven Conquerors of the Queen of the Mississippi"

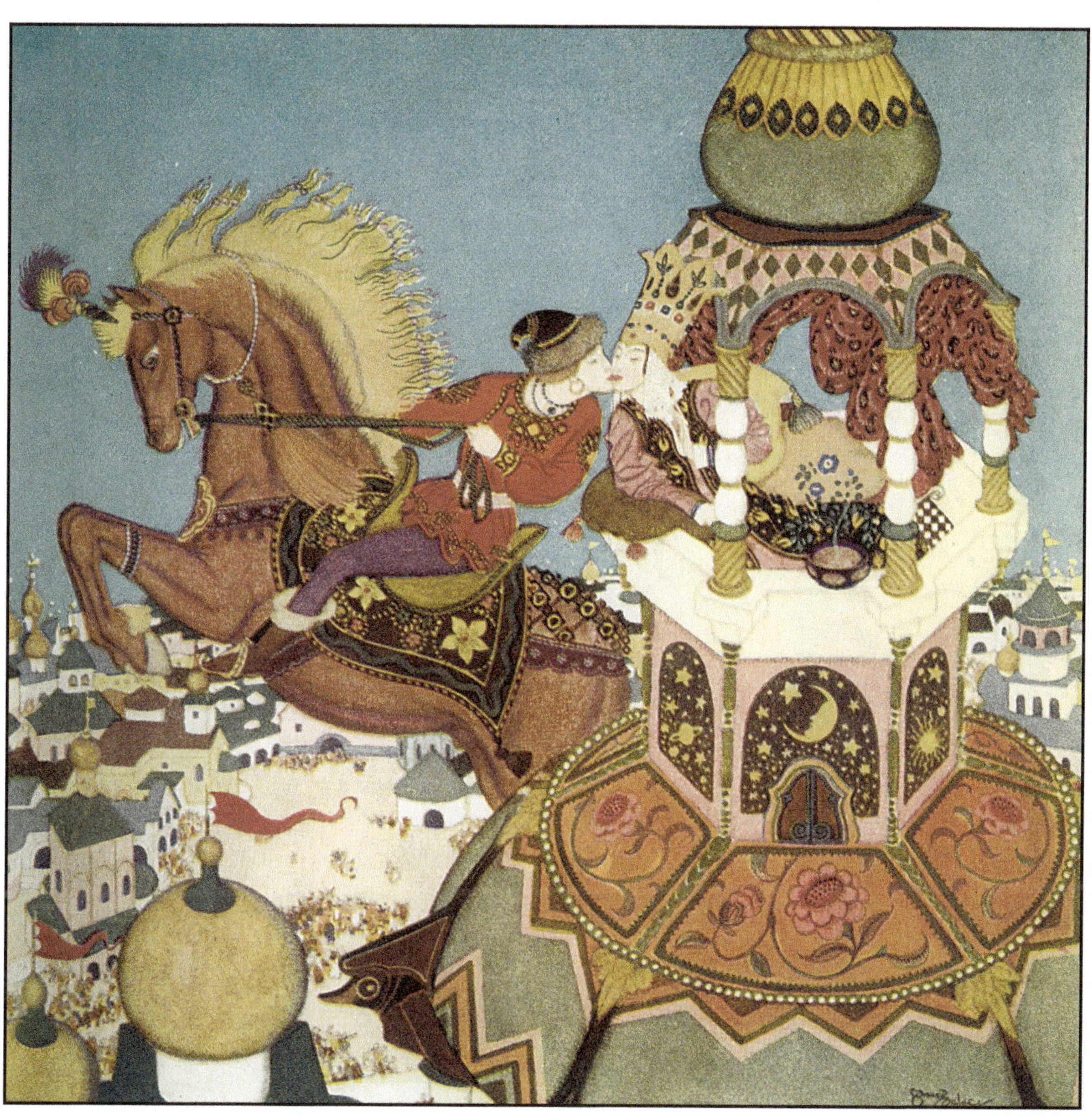

The chestnut horse seemed to linger in the air
at the top of its leap while that kiss endured.
From "Ivan and the Chestnut Horse"

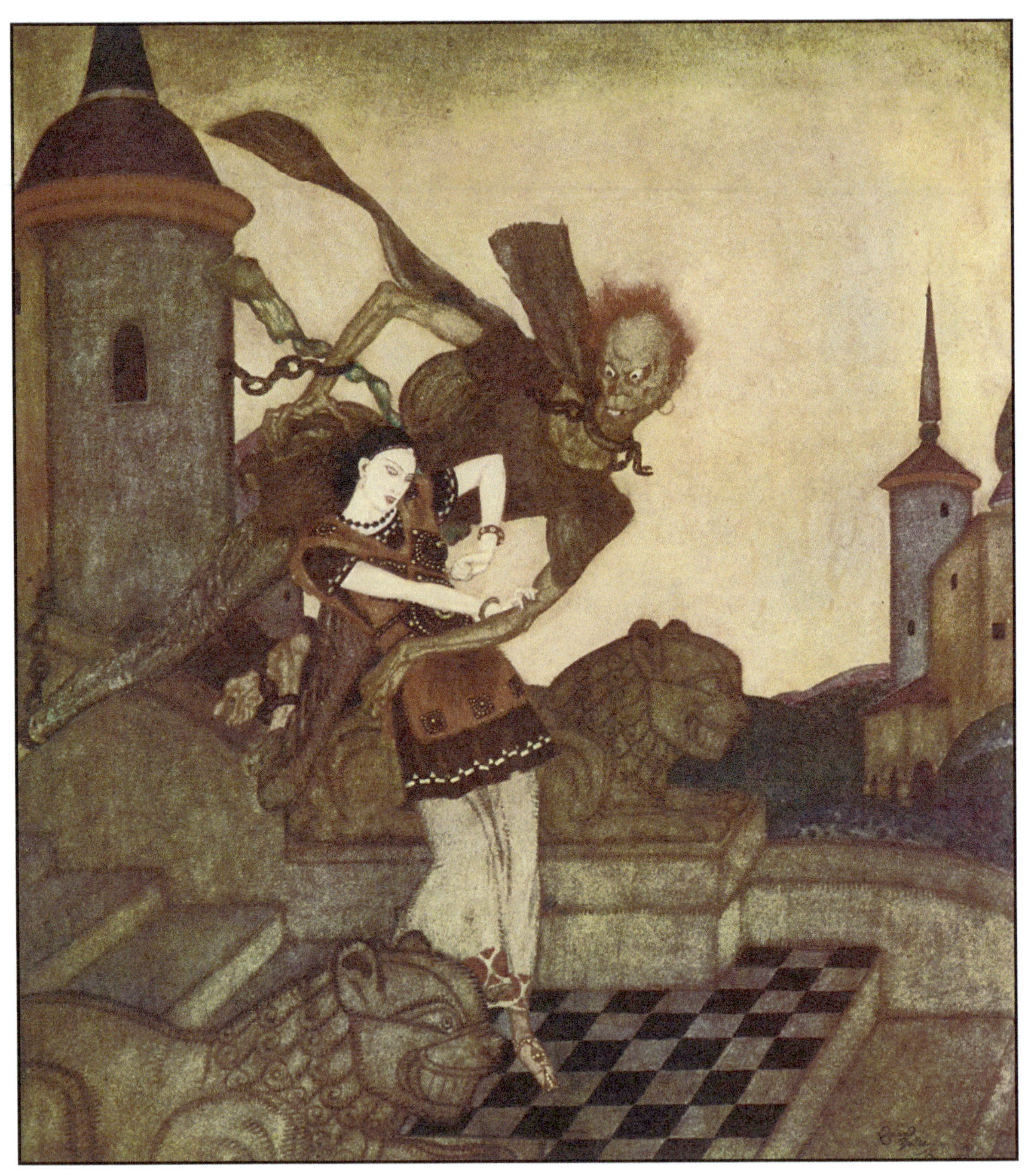

The Prince, looking out, saw him snatch up the Princess. . . .
and soar rapidly away.
From "Bashtchelik"

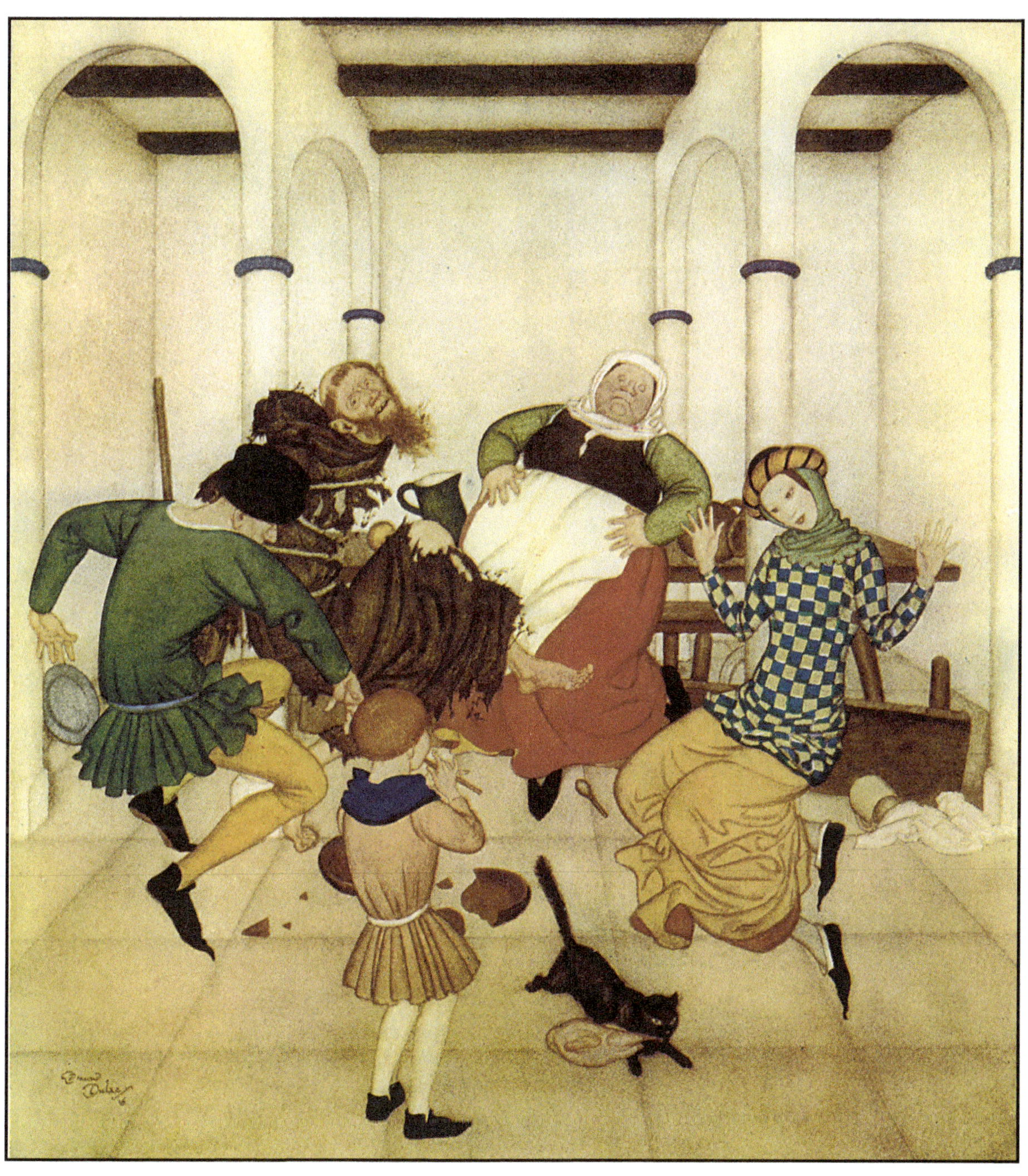

The Friar, bound fast to the post, squirmed and wriggled, showing plainly that he would foot it if he could.
From "The Friar and the Boy"

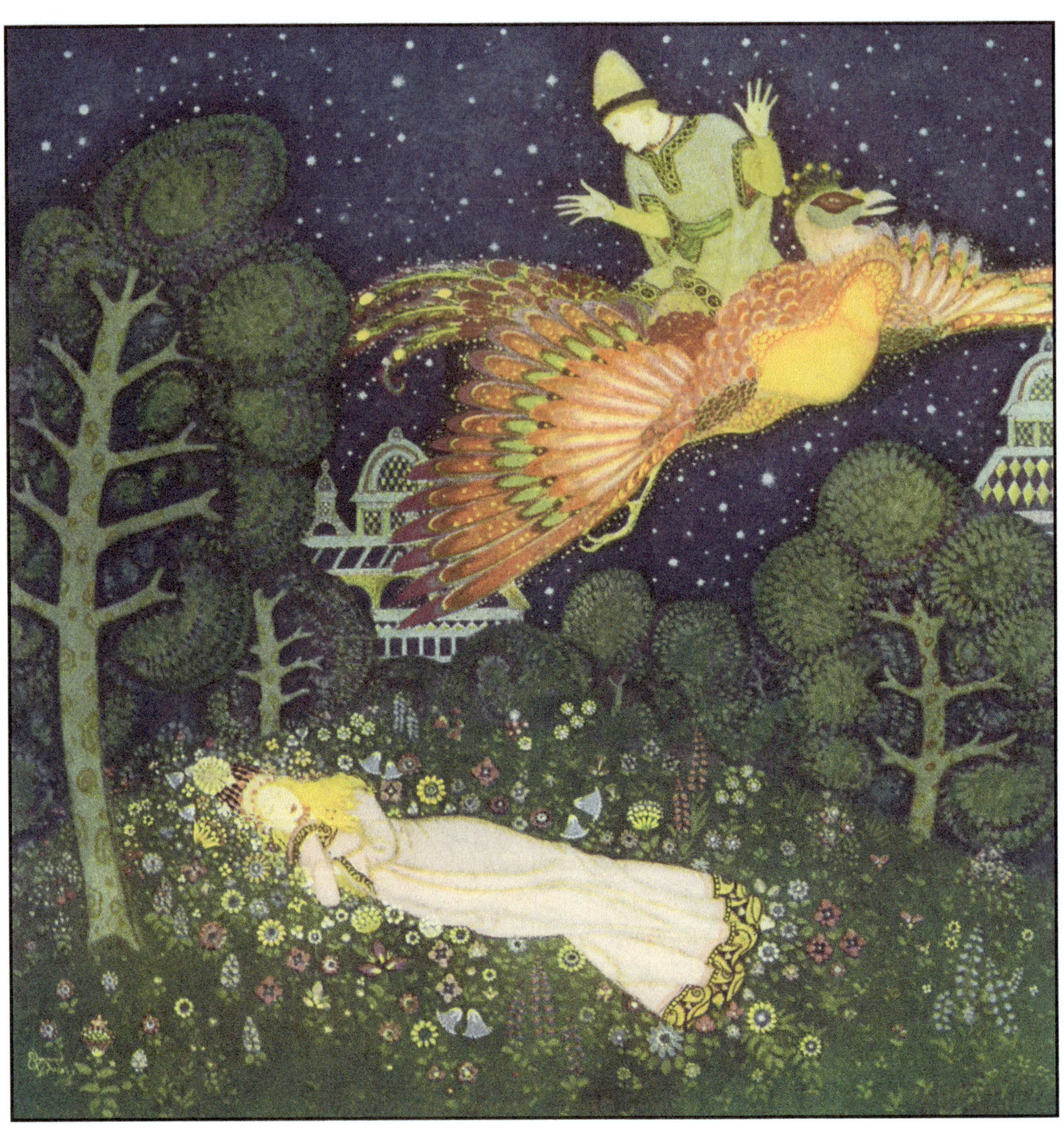

There he found the Princess asleep, and saw that her face
was the face he had seen in the portrait.
From "The Fire Bird"

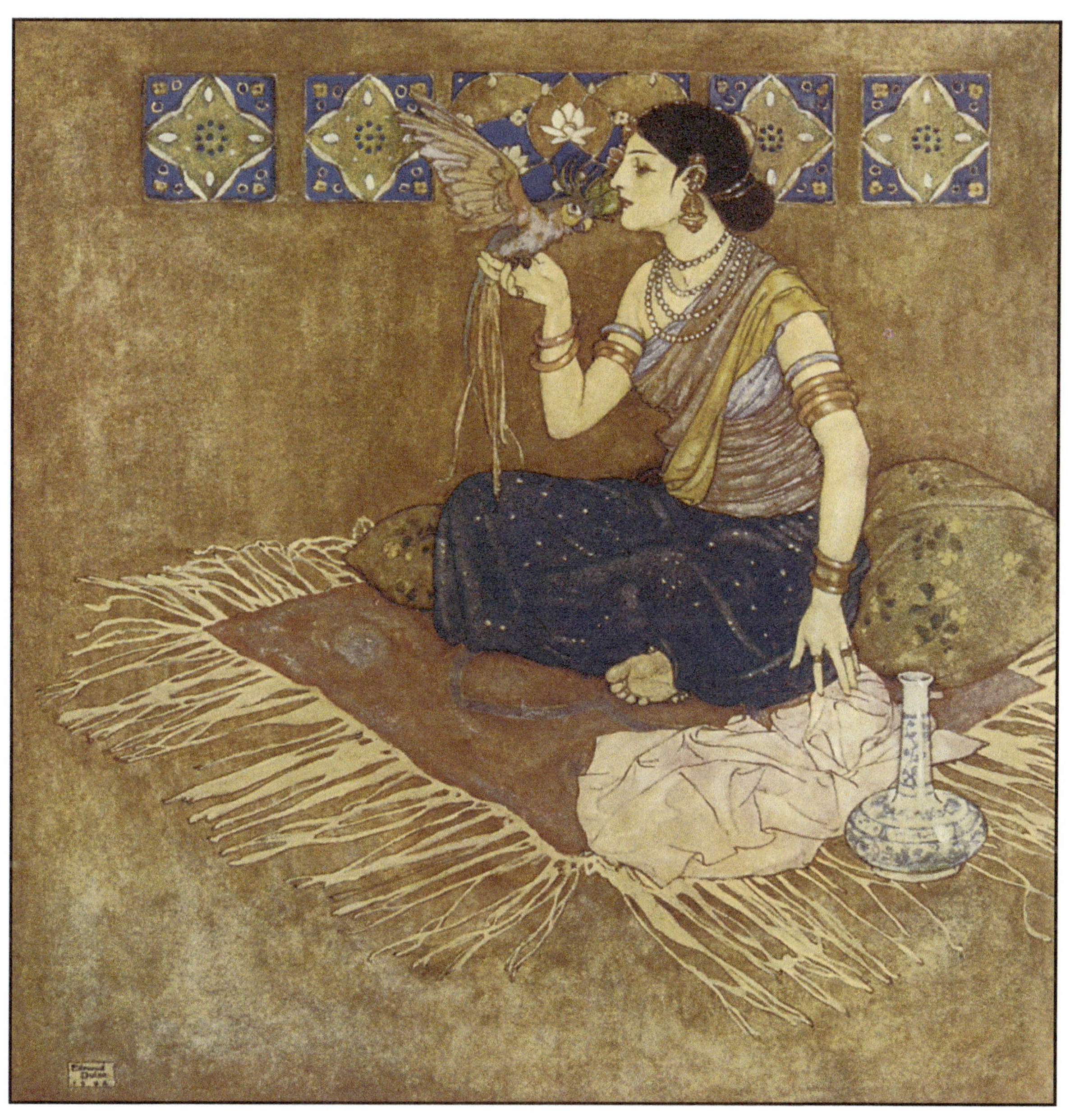

Pirouzè, the Fairest and Most Honourable Born.
From "The Story of the Wicked Half-Brothers"

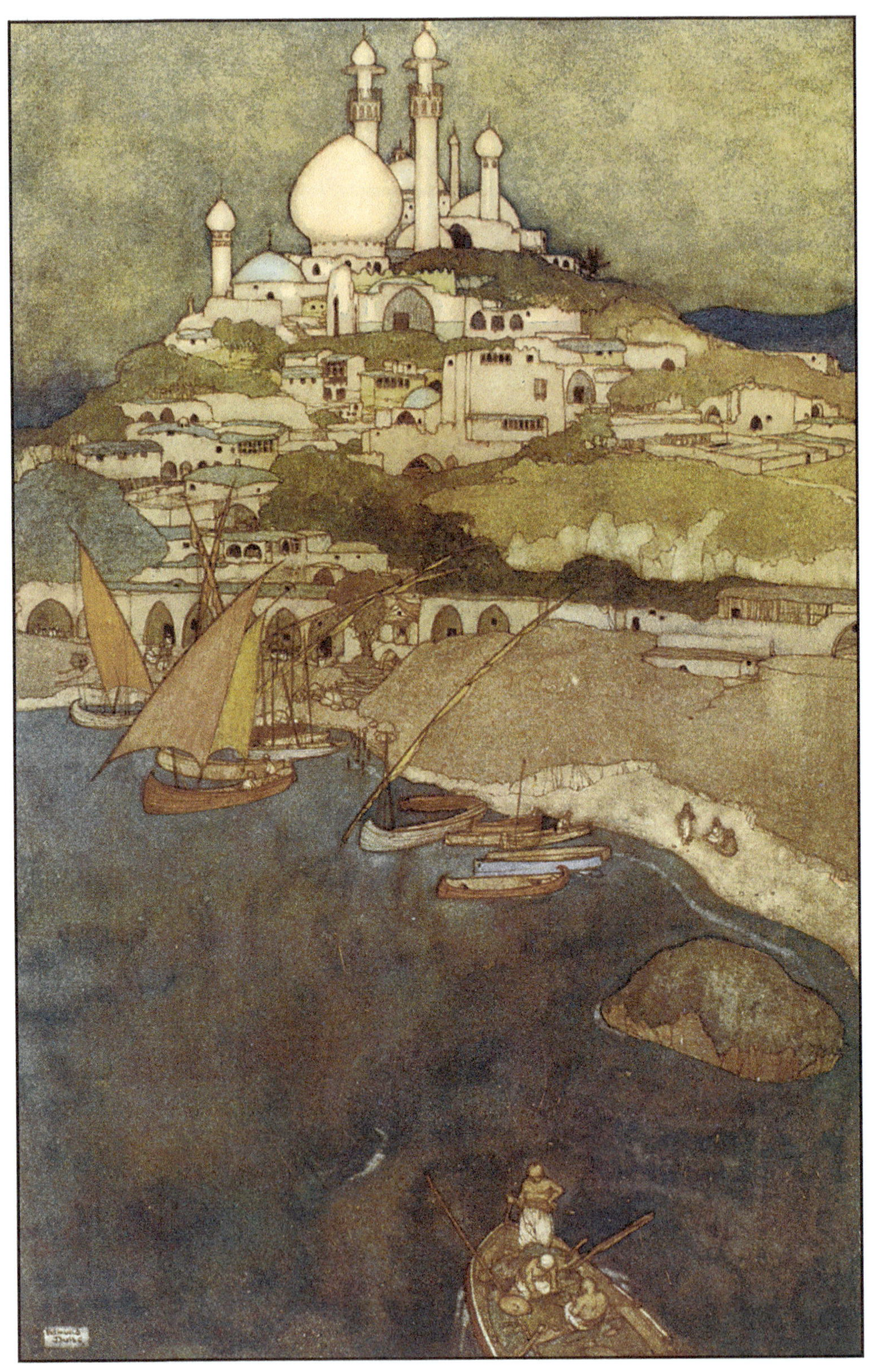

A City among the Isles named Deryabar
From "The Story of the Princess of Deryabar"

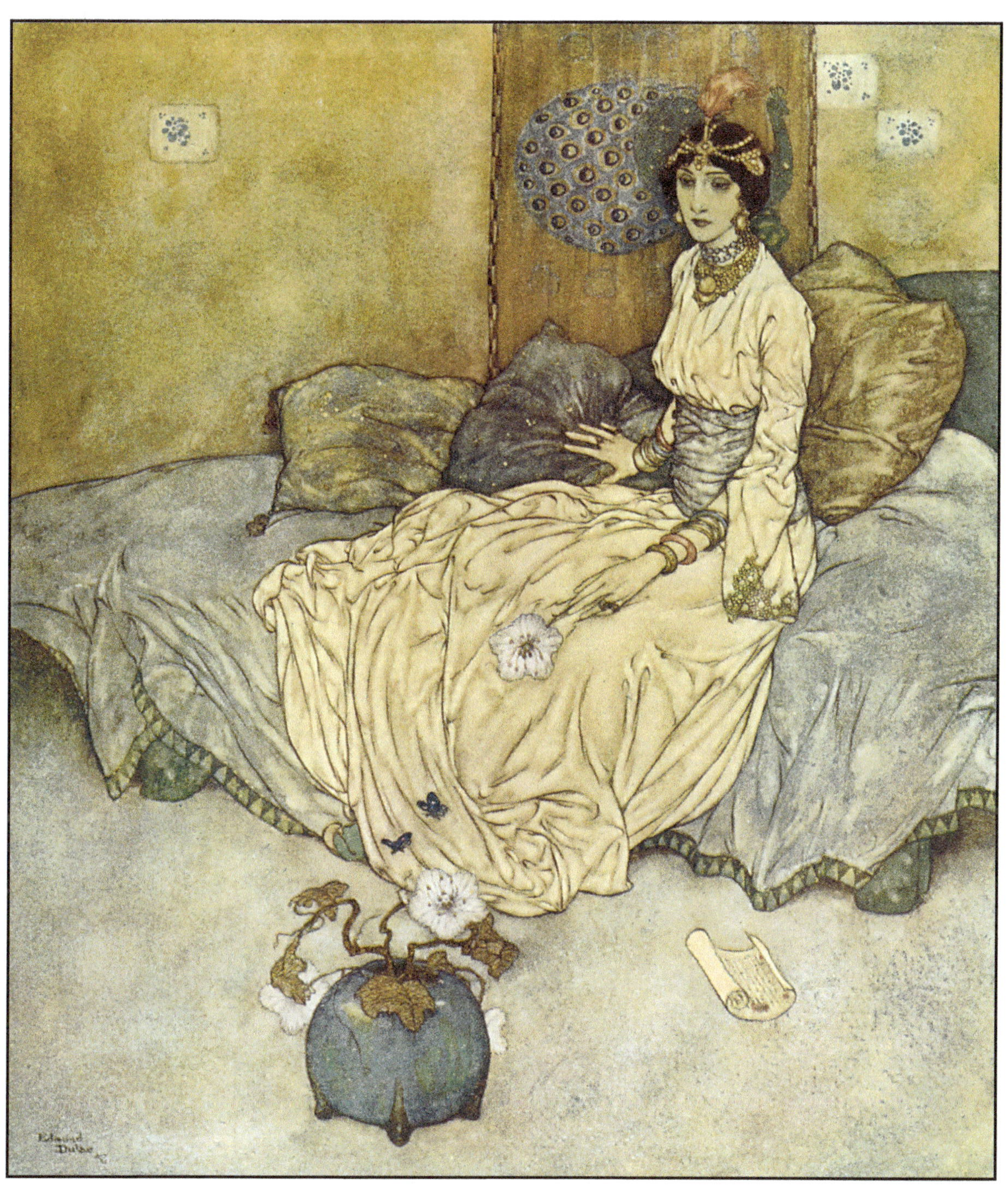

The Princess Deryabar
From "The Story of the Princess of Deryabar"

Plate 51

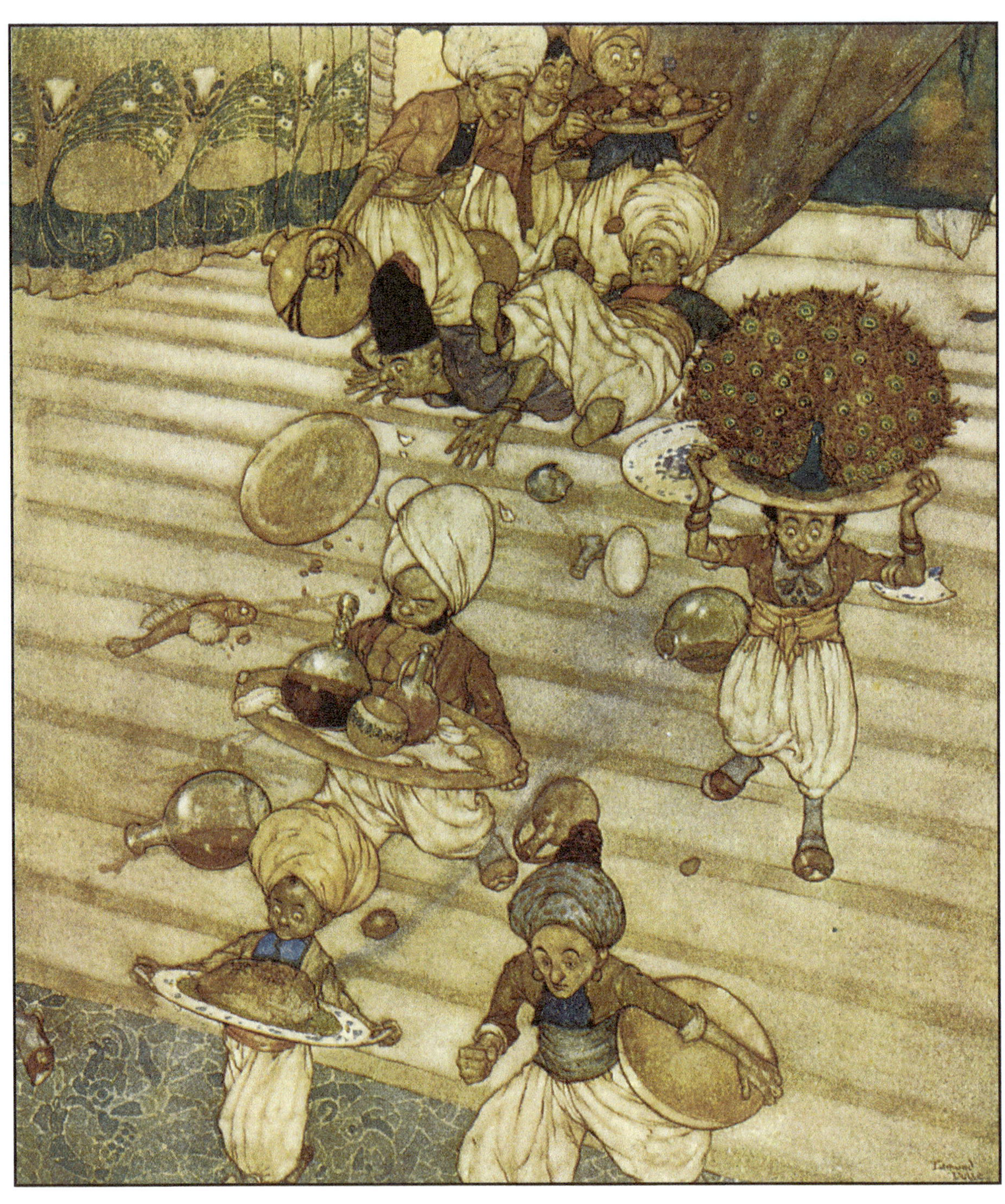

She gave orders for the banquet to be served.
From "The Magic Horse"

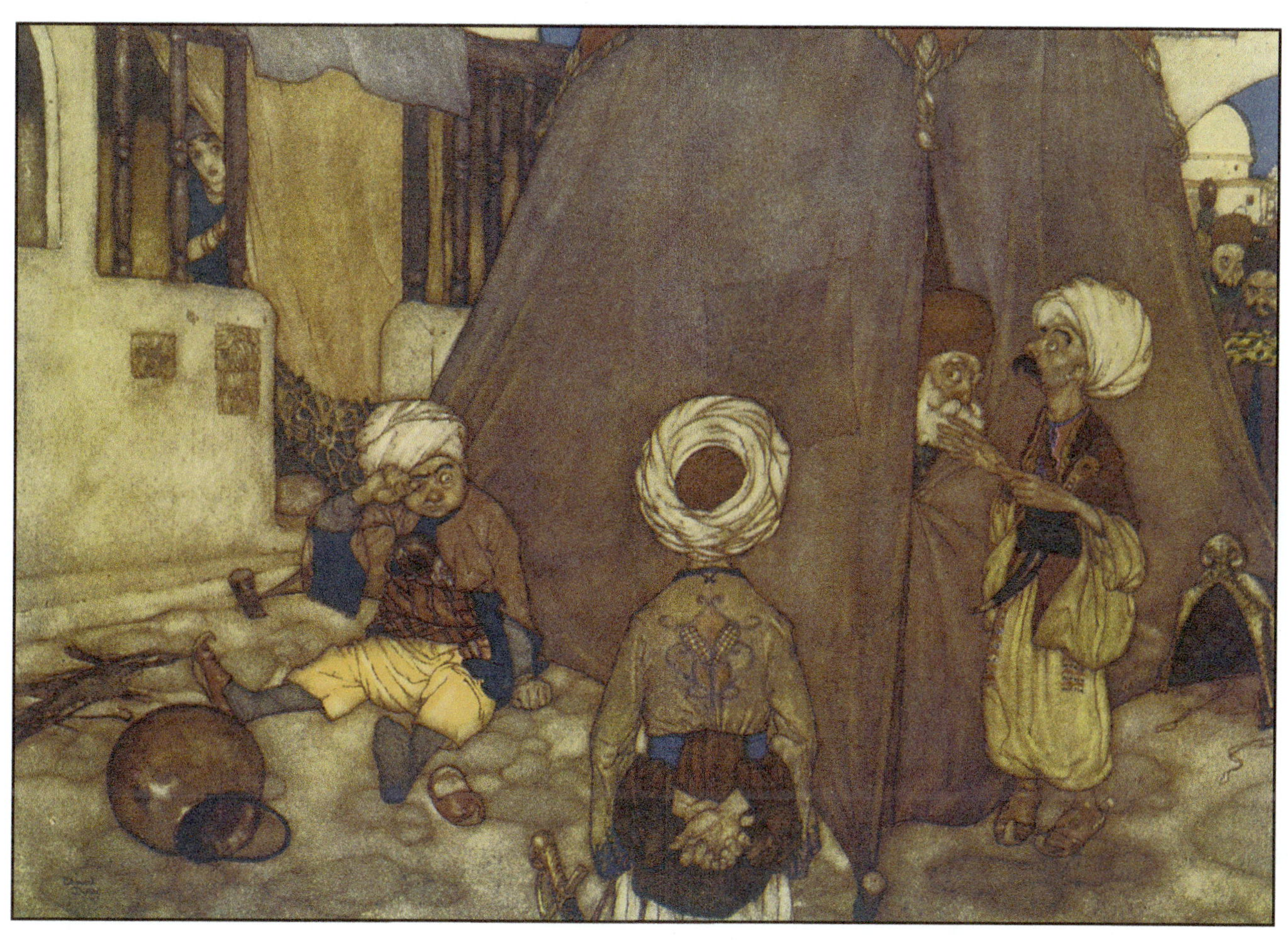

Great was the astonishment of the Vizier.
From "The King of the Ebony Isles"

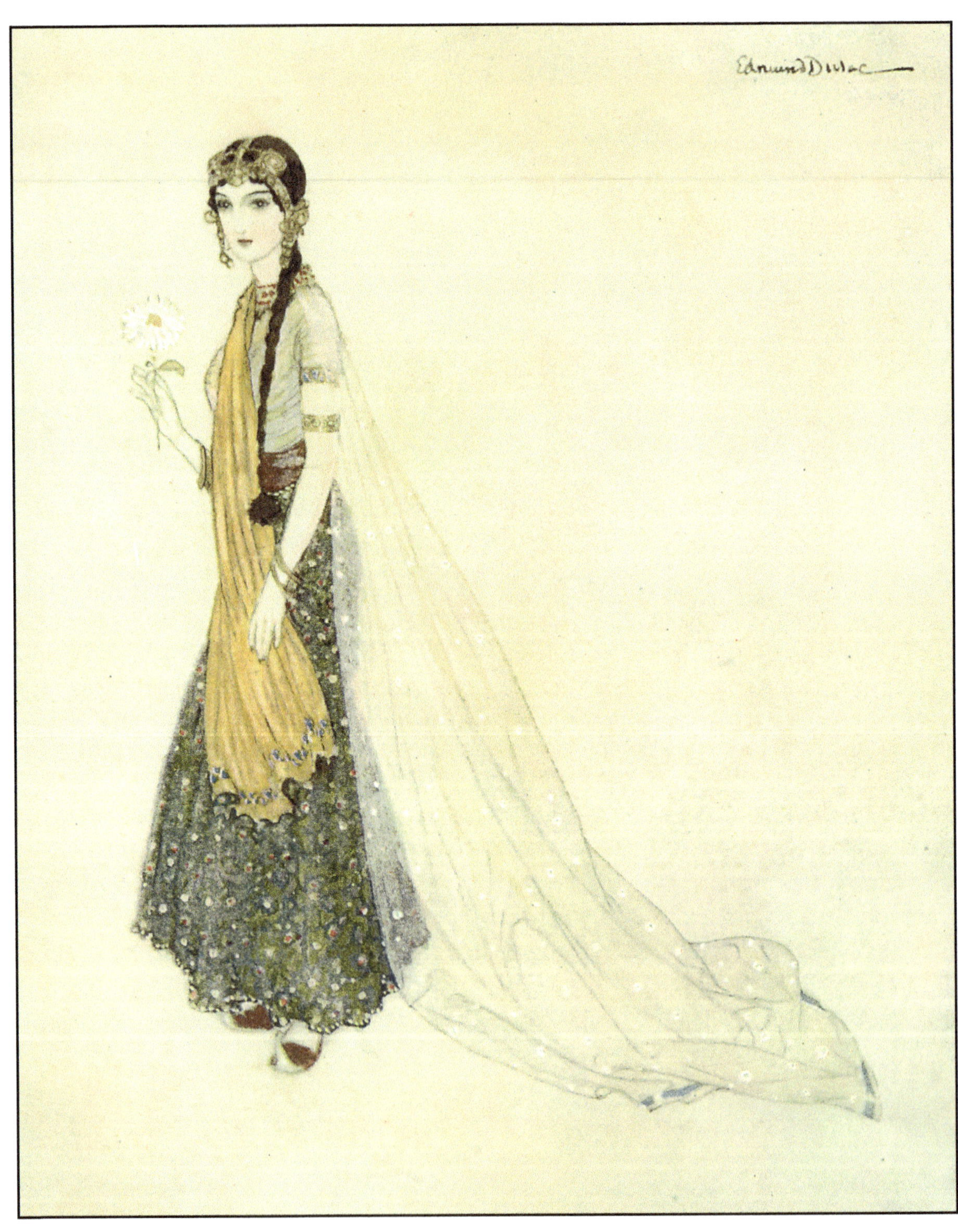

Asenath
From "Jusef and Asenath"